THE
Time
OF THE
Singing

LOUISE BLAYDON

Dreamspinner Press

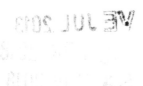

Published by
Dreamspinner Press
382 NE 191st Street #88329
Miami, FL 33179-3899, USA
http://www.dreamspinnerpress.com/

The Time of the Singing

Cover Art by Reese Dante   http://www.reesedante.com

ISBN: 978-1-61372-202-2

Printed in the United States of America
First Edition
November 2011

eBook edition available
eBook ISBN: 978-1-61372-203-9

For Jackie, a wonderful friend above and beyond the call of duty; for Jo, without whom I wouldn't quite be me; and in loving memory of my Nanna, who can be found in this book if you look hard enough.

For, lo, the winter is past, the rain is over and gone;
The flowers appear on the earth; the time of the singing is come,
And the voice of the turtledove is heard in our land.

—Song of Solomon, 2:11-12

One

THE first Mulligan Israfel meets is the youngest. It's a Sunday, his second in town, when Israfel finds him sitting on a beat-up plastic chair in the sacristy, glowering at his Game Boy. The contrast between the scowl and the pristine surplice is discordant, the combination making the boy seem simultaneously angelic and sullen. Israfel's heart sinks a little, anticipating difficulties.

Nevertheless, he puts on his best disarming smile. "Hello," he says mildly, holding out his hand. "Are you serving today? I'm sorry, I don't know your name. I'm Father Israfel."

He expects, maybe, a shrug of the shoulders and some kind of prepubescent grunt, as generally offered by the altar servers at his last parish. The smile that breaks out on the boy's face is a revelation, the firm handshake even more so. "Tom Mulligan," he returns, immediate and bright.

He's pretty, Israfel notes detachedly. In five years, he'll be gorgeous. Israfel wishes he wasn't the sort of priest to whom such realizations come naturally, but wishing has never done him very much good. It could be worse. His observations, at least, are consigned to the purely objective, constrained to innocence by the smoothness of Tom's face, his narrow, little-boy shoulders. To some men, these things would be enticements.

"Pleased to meet you, Tom," says Israfel, and means it. He half expects Tom to return to his game, let Israfel finish blessing the water and fixing his vestments, but the boy sets the Game Boy aside on an empty seat, eyebrows drawing inquisitively together.

"I like your name. Israfel's an angel, right? Like, the same as Raphael, in the Book of Enoch?"

Israfel blinks for a moment, astounded. It's literally the first time in his life that anyone has known the origin of his name, beyond vague guesses, and Tom throws out the comment like it's obvious, something he remembers from grade school. "How on earth do you know about the Book of Enoch?"

Tom shrugs, mouth tugging up at the corners, quietly pleased with himself. "I like angels. I got interested. Nate says there's no such thing, but that's just because he's a jerk."

"Is Nate a friend?"

Tom snorts and shakes his head. "He's my brother," he says, almost derisively, as if Nate is *so very much* his brother that the idea of his being anything else is laughable. "He's meant to be serving today too, but he went off somewhere. To the 'bathroom',"—Tom makes air quotes with his fingers—"except that was fifteen minutes ago and nobody takes that long to pee."

Israfel laughs softly. "Well, there's time yet. I suppose you two know what you're doing?"

"Been doing it three years," Tom returns, nodding. "Since I was ten. And Nate's been doing it since *he* was ten and he's seventeen now, so I guess you could say we pretty much have it down."

Seventeen. Israfel squares his shoulders and makes himself go on smiling, trying not to imagine what kind of seventeen-year-old this boy's brother might make. Tom's small right now, but there's height anticipated by his big feet and long legs. Any brother of his would doubtless be tall, broad in the shoulders. Tom's eyes are green, intriguing. Israfel hopes this isn't a family trait. For both their sakes, he hopes Nate is the plainer brother.

When the other boy enters the room, Israfel is straightening his vestments, back turned on the sound of approaching footsteps.

"Hey, bitchface," says the newcomer, glib and self-assured, although there's fondness under the insult.

"*Nate*," Tom hisses, scandalized, and Nate laughs.

"Sorry. Forgot you don't like to be picked on in front of servants of the Lord."

And herein, Israfel thinks, lies the trouble he'd expected when he'd first laid eyes on Tom. He finishes arranging his sash and turns around.

Nate is... definitely not the plainer brother. Tom is cute. When he grows up, he'll be extremely appealing. Nate, six feet at seventeen, is to "appealing" what the sun is to a keychain flashlight. His surplice is immaculate, stiff starched and formal, but it sits on Nate's shoulders with a kind of casual familiarity that suggests a level of ease in his own skin that Israfel has never enjoyed. Not that Israfel can blame him for it, given that Nate is far and away the most physically perfect person he's ever seen in real life. He's fairer than his brother, pale golden skin and dark golden hair, a faint constellation of freckles just visible over the bridge of his perfect nose. He does have green eyes, Israfel determines: bright, vivid green, under neatly arched brows. The line of his jaw is sharp enough to cut butter on. His mouth is as soft as sin.

Israfel is utterly undone.

Nate Mulligan is probably, Israfel thinks sadly, entirely unaware of the massive wrench he has thrown into his new padre's life by the very fact of his existence. Certainly, he holds out his (square, long-fingered) hand for Israfel to shake, as if he has no idea that all the vileness in Israfel wants to take that hand and pull him close, debauch and consume him and never let him go.

Of course he has no idea. Why should he? Priests aren't supposed to be like Israfel. Israfel is an abomination.

He bids himself be calm, takes the proffered hand and shakes it. His voice, when it emerges—"Hello, Nate. Good to meet you. I've just been talking to your brother, here."—is perfectly steady, revealing nothing. Israfel is twenty-nine years old, and he has been concealing himself from the world since he was fourteen. Fifteen years of practice, it seems, can help a man cope with challenges that once would have been insurmountable.

"Sorry about him," Nate says and laughs. Israfel feels an absurd urge to lick the boy's (perfect) teeth, abruptly followed by a surge of guilt that shoots hot through his jaw like a vein of molten silver.

"Not at all," Israfel protests, and the fact that his voice continues to be even is nothing short of astonishing. He smooths his sash, fussily and unnecessarily. His palms are damp against the cloth. "He was very illuminating."

Nate laughs again and clicks his tongue. "Oh, I bet. Trash talking me to the new priest already, huh, Tommy?"

Tom crosses his arms and tosses his head in a gesture several years too old for his childish frame, eyebrows raised scornfully. "Was *not*. Believe it or not, I do have better things to talk about, Nate. And it's *Tom*."

"Oh, right. Of course. I forgot about how you're all grown up now." Nate shoots out an arm, curls it around his brother's head, and drags him into something that might have been a headlock but could equally just be an attempt to smother Tom with his armpit. It's immature and rough, and Tom's protesting vehemently while he pummels Nate with his far-smaller fists, but there's nothing but fondness in it, really, and both of them are laughing as they grapple.

The foolish, *obscene* twist of jealousy in Israfel's gut is simply further evidence of the true hopelessness of his situation. He is a grown man—a man of the cloth, moreover, sworn husband to the Church of Christ and no other—and he's envious of the thirteen-year-old whose face is currently smushed into Nate Mulligan's armpit.

"Holy Mary, pray for us sinners," he mutters in a voice inaudible to earthly ears as he heads out into the sanctuary.

It doesn't do much to reassure him, but currently, it's the best plan he has.

The Mulligan boys serve the Mass more efficiently than anyone Israfel's ever worked with before, even including the fifteen-year-old girl in Illinois who'd spoken to him about entering a convent. These boys serve as if they've known this service about as long as they've known language, and as far as Israfel knows, it could be true. Their matching expressions of quiet devotion make him smile a little as he circulates the chalice, remembering the way they'd teased each other earlier, irreverent and carefree. They're both evidently anxious to display their devotion to their work.

When he meets their parents, when the Mass has been served and the congregation is filing past him into the graveyard, Israfel has a better understanding of *why*. The boys disappear back into the sacristy to put things away and change back into their own clothes, which takes long enough that Mr. and Mrs. Mulligan are required to hang back from the line to wait for them, making them readily identifiable. By the time the little family reaches Israfel at the door, the church is empty, the smell of incense headier in the silence that's fallen.

"Mr. and Mrs. Mulligan, I presume," Israfel says, putting on his most inviting smile as he holds out his hand for them to take.

Mr. Mulligan's grip is strong, insistent. There's something militaristic in his bearing too, and both things together suggest some time in armed service. His free hand is clasped on Tom's shoulder, but it isn't a reassuring touch, nor a particularly friendly one. It's a firm hand, rather, as if he feels that his youngest son is somehow in need of stern handling, and the picture they make is altogether too familiar. Israfel has known a lot of "firm-hand" fathers in his time in the ministry, all of them reminiscent of his own.

The gruff voice is absolutely in accord with the man. "John Mulligan," he says, and then, "and it's Captain."

Israfel isn't sure whether to congratulate himself on his fine deductive reasoning or flush at being so pointedly corrected. In the end, he simply smiles awkwardly, and John obligingly continues, unabated.

"Good to meet you, Father; good to meet you. I hope my boys here didn't give you any grief?"

Israfel laughs and shakes his head. "They're extraordinarily well behaved. The best altar servers I've ever had the pleasure of working with, in fact. You should be proud."

"Oh, we *are*."

Mrs. Mulligan's tone leaves Israfel in no doubt as to her sincerity, even if her husband's white-knuckled grip leaves him questioning. She's slightly built and blonde and evidently the source of her eldest son's good looks. She delicately declines to shake Israfel's outstretched hand—an affectation Israfel has rarely seen in women below the age of seventy—but her smile is very genuine and oddly familiar.

"And I should hope they do serve a perfect Mass. We always run through it in Saturday-morning school, before we study the catechism, so there's no excuse not to. Is there?" She grins sidelong at her eldest son, squeezing his hand affectionately.

"None," Nate tells her flatly. He's looking at the ground, patient but rather expressionless. Israfel finds himself wishing the boy would look up, but admittedly it is probably for the best that he doesn't.

"Do you teach a special Saturday class, then, Mrs. Mulligan?" he asks, politely inquisitive.

"Lynda, please." Lynda smiles at him, and it's Nate's smile, straight-toothed and compelling. "I homeschool them, actually; I trained as a teacher, but obviously, after these two came along...." She laughs and spreads her hands, as if the rest is self-explanatory—as indeed it is. Lynda Mulligan is clearly a very conservative Roman Catholic. Israfel wonders if this is the general attitude in this parish—that married women ought not to work outside of the home—or if she is simply exceptionally pious. His last parish had been rather lenient on such matters.

"She's a marvel," John puts in, his tone fond but rather brusque. Israfel recognizes it immediately. It is undoubtedly the tone of a man eager to quiet his wife before she can launch into a twenty-minute narrative about a subject in which he is entirely uninterested. He reaches over Tom's head for Lynda's hand, squeezes, and tugs, his intention unmistakable. "Aren't you?"

Lynda laughs. "Whatever you say, hon."

Israfel has seen many women hold firm under this kind of attack, stubbornly continuing their anecdotes while their husbands pull on their arms with an increasing lack of subtlety. Lynda Mulligan is evidently not that sort of woman. She takes the hint gracefully, obediently, lacing her fingers through John's and turning toward the door. "It was lovely to meet you, Father. I hope you'll be very happy here."

"Bless you," Israfel says vaguely as they file out. The boys are quiet, scuffing their sneakers as they follow their parents out into the sunlit churchyard. Israfel remembers the way they were in the sacristy, both of them outspoken and laughing. For a moment, the contrast gives him pause.

Then he thinks about Lynda's face, the look of quiet pride when she spoke of her sons. No trace of a sign of anything there but love and the passing on of piety. They're a normal family, two boys and their good Catholic parents. Homeschooling isn't something Israfel has come across before, but that doesn't permit him to be prejudiced against it. Everybody knows the public school system is a joke, and a Godless one, at that. If Israfel had children, he might well want to teach them himself, given the extortionate fees Catholic schools charge.

But Israfel has no children and never will. He has his flock, his duties, and his prayers. His vows make him a shepherd and a son but forbid him the path of fatherhood.

The cross of the Mass is heavy around Israfel's neck, solid and cool when he closes his fingers around it. It is his protection, his security, and his guide. Sometimes, Israfel stands like this before the mirror, reminds himself that this is what the whole world sees. Here is a man removed from normality by his own choice, by the strength of his love of God. He denies himself the pleasures of women because Paul commanded it, and through fidelity to the Holy Roman Church. In another life, Father Israfel could have been anyone, a lover and a husband and a father.

Sometimes, Israfel can almost believe the lie.

But then there are boys like Nate Mulligan, young and strong and so beautiful that Israfel can *feel* the flames. Pure sons of pious families, and the evil in Israfel yearns to smear its filth all over them.

Israfel is a blind man leading the blind, and sometimes it is hard to forget it. It is a sin to bear false witness, and he is sinning every day of his life.

There are greater sins. Israfel envisages them in Nate Mulligan's mouth, in all the smooth lines of his body.

As consolation goes, it isn't the best, but Israfel's used to that. For years, he has plodded on as the lesser of two evils.

Nate isn't the first boy to have moved him to lust and frustration and anguish. There is no reason why he has to be any different than all the ones who have come before.

This is a lie, of course, but Israfel is used to that and has his ways around it.

He prescribes himself a hundred Hail Marys and fumbles out his rosary. The words trip over his tongue half-felt, familiar, and by the time he has prayed ten, Nate Mulligan is out of his mind, Israfel untouchable like this, wrapped in his endless circle of prayer.

He tidies the sanctuary as he prays, then retreats to the rectory. There's half a bottle of sacramental wine left over. He sets it on the side table as he enters the house and *looks* at it.

He has to drink it. The Church is very clear on this question. "This is my blood, poured out for many." To fail to consume the sacrament is a grave blasphemy, and Israfel wouldn't dream of it. The congregation had been unusually small this morning, though, a lot of families out of town for the Labor Day weekend, and the resultant leftovers are correspondingly great. Probably, he should dispose of the wine in small amounts, rationed throughout the day.

By two in the afternoon, the bottle is entirely empty, Israfel's duty fulfilled. The room is swimming around him, the quantity of alcohol unfamiliar and affecting him overmuch, but his mind is blissfully empty.

It will be all right, he thinks. Everything has always been all right before.

Two

ON MONDAY morning, Israfel wakes at five. There's an early Latin Mass on Mondays and Thursdays, and Israfel, as much a scholar as a priest, rather looks forward to it. His previous parish had been smaller and far less well attended and had not offered either Latin Mass or a full-sung Eucharist. This church, contrarily, indulges itself in tradition wherever it can, and Israfel delights in it. He would have been happy to chant the service even into an empty seven o'clock void. It is beyond pleasing that there are actually people here at this hour to listen as he declaims the ancient words. It isn't exactly a full house, but fifteen people is an excellent turnout for this kind of service, and Israfel glows with it.

He hopes it isn't too obvious, as he steps up to the altar, that his enjoyment of the Latin is almost indecent. He should not, perhaps, be smiling as the words trip transcendent from his tongue, but he can't seem to help it. Like this, he feels that he is speaking the language of the Lord, that the angels must truly be listening. It's a baseless feeling, he knows. It isn't as if he really thinks that God speaks Latin, but nevertheless, he can't shake it. The *confiteor* in the Latin feels like exorcism, like uplifting his heart to be cleansed.

Confiteor Deo omnipotenti, beatae Mariae semper Virgini, beato Michaeli Archangelo, beato Joanni Baptistae, sanctis Apostolis Petro et Paulo, omnibus Sanctis, et vobis fratres, quia peccavi nimis cogitatione, verbo, et opere: mea culpa, mea culpa, mea maxima culpa. Ideo precor beatam Mariam semper Virginem, beatum Michaelem Archangelum, beatum Joannem Baptistam, sanctos Apostolos Petrum et Paulum, omnes Sanctos, et vos fratres, orare pro me ad Dominum Deum nostrum.

They will pray for him, he thinks, the host of saints and angels, and his sins of thought and word and deed are confessed. As the words roll out of him, a little of his guilt rolls with them, until he is so light that it's vertiginous. This, he thinks, is why he loves the Church; this euphoria and a Mass that feels like spell work.

The Brethren wish Israfel God's forgiveness, and he luxuriates for a moment in it, loving the sound of the Latin, like benediction or magic. He likes this parish, and the parishioners like him. He will fit in here. Everything will be fine.

It *will*. Israfel has faith.

FOR six days, everything is. Israfel visits elderly ladies and mothers with new babies, watches the bell ringers with interest when they practice in the belfry, and presides over coffee mornings for older people. This is a sleepy parish, old-fashioned and quiet in an autumnal, New Englandish way, and Israfel *loves* it.

On the seventh day, God rested, but Israfel cannot.

The average age of a congregation goes a long way toward determining what activities are provided, and Israfel's is a little over middle-aged, all told. Consequently, Israfel finds his schedule filled with things that women over forty might enjoy but is not called upon to operate a Sunday school. What children there are in the church seem to be educated in the catechism by their parents.

Israfel is used to having his altar servers be older people for midweek Masses, but ordinarily, the list of teenagers forced by their parents into serving on Sundays is long. In his last post—already beginning to feel like another life—Israfel had been required to devise a sort of rota, allotting Sundays to volunteers over a six- or seven-week period. In this town, things are far simpler. The first and third Sundays of the month are served, without exception, by the Mulligan boys. Alternate Sundays fall to Anne Thompson and Jessica Dobson, who served the Mass his first Sunday presiding. The Mulligans, Israfel recognized belatedly, had not been there that week, perhaps out of town for some reason.

This week, the Mulligans are very much present.

Anne and Jess, while less adept than Tom and Nate, certainly know the service to the letter and perform their required tasks without any interference from Israfel. Israfel is grateful to be able to leave these things to trust. There's nothing worse than attempting to give a heartfelt sermon through a niggling sense that the altar servers are about to inadvertently set the sanctuary alight. Today, Israfel has prepared a homily based upon the life of the apostle Mark, which he is more than a little proud of, and he looks forward to delivering it in good form. Mark is, after all, his favorite.

At least it can be said that he begins well. The congregation seems to have taken to him, Israfel is pleased to note, and their attentive faces do much for his confidence. "We are never," he begins, "so close to Jesus as we are brought through the good news of the Gospels. This is most true of Mark's Gospel, which…."

Oration is one of the skills in which every seminarian is trained, and Israfel has always been especially good at it. He knows as well as anyone that eye contact is one of the simplest and most useful things an orator can do to engage people's interest, and an interested congregation makes the difference between a good homilist and a bad one. Israfel's homily is well rehearsed, and he lets his gaze travel over the faces of his parishioners as he speaks, easy and assuring.

He doesn't know all their names yet, but, with all the fervor of a young priest with his first full parish, he most certainly means to. He tests himself in his head as he scans the second row of pews, naming those he can and mentally marking those he can't to speak to later, so that he'll remember them next Sunday. The old woman at the end of the row is one of the sacristans, Mrs. King. Her husband is seated to her left, and then Mr. and Mrs. O'Donnell with their new baby (blissfully quiet). Beyond them is a single woman in her thirties, whose name Israfel does not know, and then—he has to drop his gaze a few inches—Tom Mulligan. He appears to be finding his knees terribly interesting, for which Israfel can't really blame him—even if the only interesting thing about Tom Mulligan's knees is that they are bare, because his parents seem to believe in the archaic custom of shorts-on-Sunday-until-you-grow. Teenagers don't listen to homilies unless they have vocations, and Israfel doesn't hold it against them.

So when Israfel's eyes drift on over to Tom's left and alight immediately upon Nate's, he's a little surprised. Every other person in the church below the age of twenty-five appears to be studying the floor, but Nate Mulligan—beautiful Nate, with his angel face that brings out all the evil in Israfel—is staring straight back at him.

It's a little disconcerting.

"It's possible," Israfel hears himself saying, "it's... *possible*... I mean... some scholars believe that we do get... get a *glimpse* of Mark in his own Gospel, um. That he writes himself in, as it were, like Vonnegut."

The little ripple of amusement that spreads through the church at that makes Israfel feel a little better about the stumble, but his cheeks still feel overheated. He is speaking, for goodness' sake, and Nate is looking at him. The concurrence of events is hardly unprecedented. He ought to be *pleased*.

He *ought*, in fact, to be looking somewhere in the region of Mrs. Elliott on the far side of the pew by now, but for some reason, he is still staring straight at Nate, as if waiting for the boy to break eye contact before he can tear his eyes away. Nate's not doing anything except look, but his eyes are so steady, so endlessly, emphatically green, that Israfel cannot bring himself to forsake them. The thought crosses his mind that it must feel rather like this to be in thrall, as in the old stories. He is still speaking, and he knows that his voice is even and measured, that his words are emerging exactly as intended, but the homily is an afterthought, now, nothing but a footnote to the all-consuming Book of Nate. It's ridiculous, but the thought of moving on rings an ache in Israfel's head, a promise of pain.

And then Nate moves.

It isn't, to be honest, the sort of movement that would be obvious to anyone else, unless they, too, were fixated on his face. Israfel cannot understand why *everyone* in the church is not fixated on Nate's face, but then, he supposes, most people are less easily drawn than he is. As it is, he can see nobody else watching and must presume that the quirk of Nate's eyebrow, the slow, lopsided smile, are for him alone. Nate's face goes from studious to smirking in the space of a second, and Israfel's cheeks are already heating with it when Nate puts out his tongue—not ostentatiously, but as if inconsequentially, naturally—and wets his lips.

It's only a flash of pink on pink and a shimmer of lingering dampness, but Nate is still looking right at him, and Israfel is abruptly, shamefully, half-hard.

He jerks his eyes away, heart thundering in his chest, and struggles wildly for speech.

"Of course the, um, the, the disciples of Jesus, those who were... who were with him on his ministry..."

It's a good save because Israfel is a good speaker, and the congregation doesn't seem to have noticed, but Israfel knows, can still feel beneath his cassock the heat engendered by his treacherous thoughts. For a moment, he is blindingly, terrifyingly sure that Nate Mulligan somehow knows his secret, that the boy is toying with him with intent.

When, ten minutes later, he dares a glance back at Nate, he finds him kicking surreptitiously at his brother's feet, the two of them grinning at each other with their heads ducked. Everything about his posture is innocent and young, and Israfel immediately feels wrong on every level, not only feeling these things for this boy, but trying to thrust the blame upon his shoulders. Nate is just a boy whose face has probably caused him enough trouble as it is. The last thing he needs is to be saddled with Israfel's desires and mistaken assumptions and fears.

After the service, Israfel is unexpectedly overtaken by a blinding headache. He cannot *possibly* stay to wish the congregation well. He is terribly sorry, but he's sure his deacon will perform the task very well on his own.

Israfel retreats to the rectory like a deserter gone to ground and buries his face in his pillow.

Three

THE following Tuesday evening, Nate shows up for bell ringing. Given that Nate has never shown the slightest interest in campanology, this leaves Israfel rather surprised. He glances at Ricky, the instructor and organist, in search of enlightenment—perhaps Nate has been a regular bell ringer in the past?—but the look on Ricky's face clearly conveys his equal bemusement.

"Nate," says Israfel, wondering where to begin.

"Since when do you give a damn about the bells?" demands Ricky, who seems to be without compunction.

Nate laughs and shrugs his shoulders, both hands stuffed into the pockets of his jeans. They're rather tight jeans, so "stuffed" really is the only word.

"I like the bells," Nate protests, eyebrows raised in appeal. Israfel wishes he found it half so easy to resist as Ricky seems to.

"Uh-huh," Ricky retorts dryly. "Well, it's the middle of the season, Nate. I only take on new folks at Michaelmas and Easter, you know that as well as anyone. And you've never cared." He leans forward, eyes narrowed skeptically. "Why're you really here, Mulligan?"

It occurs to Israfel, as he watches this little scene play out, that Ricky seems to know a side of Nate that his parents aren't privy to. The tone of Ricky's voice suggests that he's dealing fondly, but firmly, with a known troublemaker, which was not Lynda's attitude at all. Then again, Ricky speaks to a lot of people like that.

"I just want to listen, Ricky," Nate insists, although Israfel notices that he cuts back a little on the wide-eyed innocence. "If it's not too much of a problem for you?"

The skepticism in Ricky's face shows no sign of diminishing, but he tightens his lips in reluctant acquiescence before turning back to take hold of his bell rope. "Fine. Stay and watch, and I hope the music's pretty enough for you, but you stay out of my way, you got it?"

"Got it, Ricky," Nate retorts happily. Casually, he leans back against the dilapidated piano, spread-eagling his arms across the top of it. It's mild out, and they're bare, the shadows of muscles visible under the skin. Israfel clears his throat.

"Thanks, Ricky. Do you want to try that last one again?"

Ricky snorts. "Well, we'll just have to, won't we? Since we were so rudely interrupted." He gestures at the ringers, waits a moment before counting them all back in. "On three, Alison, that's you—"

Nate shakes his head and smiles at Israfel sidelong. "*Ricky,*" he says, with that same exasperated fondness. "*You* don't mind that I came to listen, do you? I love the sound of church bells. And it's never so good from the outside as it sounds when you're right up against it." He grins. "I like to be, you know, right inside."

The downward flicker of his eyes is barely perceptible. Israfel is probably imagining it.

"I don't mind at all," Israfel assures, smiling briefly at Nate before turning his head to stare very fixedly at the back of Ricky's neck. Nate's shirt is rather close cut, broad chest thrust outward by his crucifixion stance only straining the cotton further. Israfel can't look at him, so he won't. This is how Israfel survives.

Nate Mulligan, it seems, does not have Israfel's survival at the forefront of his interests.

"So… you liking it here?" He leans his head back and rolls it, as if the muscles in his neck are tight from exertion, and ends the motion with his head on one shoulder, looking down the length of his arm at Israfel.

Israfel smiles, a little tight lipped, and keeps his eyes on Ricky. Unfortunately, his peripheral vision is good, and Nate is close enough that the general stance and movement of his body are perceptible, even when Israfel looks straight ahead, and he can hardly justify actively turning his head away. "I love it," he says, cautiously but truthfully. "I'm an old-fashioned sort of priest, in many ways, and this is kind of an old-fashioned parish. I'd never have had an opportunity to read a Latin Mass at my last church, for example."

Nate raises his eyebrows, lips pursed curiously. Israfel shoots him a brief glance, long enough to notice once again just how singular those lips are, and then quickly looks away again.

"You like the Latin Mass, huh?" Nate sounds genuinely intrigued. "I've never been to one. Languages are more Tommy's thing, 'specially dead ones."

Israfel smiles at that, the throwaway comment going some distance toward setting him at his ease. "Is he the scholarly type, then, your brother?"

"Is he the nerdy one, you mean?" Nate laughs. "Yeah, for sure. Guess he's the brains in our family, and I'm the beauty, huh?"

Israfel opens his mouth, heat seizing up the muscles at the top of his spine, and then closes it again. There is really no response he can give to that without sounding as if he is perversely attracted to either Nate (true, but not to be discussed) or Tom (untrue, but far more dangerous), and Israfel suspects Nate knows it. At any rate, Nate doesn't wait for a response but runs his thumb over the top of Israfel's shoulder through the cassock before returning his eyes to the bell ringers.

Israfel feels the touch like a slow burn.

For a while, they listen in a silence that swiftly becomes companionable, once Israfel overcomes the sense of being oddly short of breath. Ricky is certainly good at what he does, and the bells are old and sound, their song clear and strong. Bell ringing is as much a full-body exercise as a musical endeavor, though, and practice can only go on for so long. Eventually, Ricky steps back from his rope, flexing his fingers where they've cramped up like claws around the bellpull.

"Okay, kids," he calls.

The middle-aged man next to him—Israfel believes his name is Caleb—lets go of his own bellpull and grins. "Kid yourself," he mutters in Ricky's direction.

"I'm in charge, ain't I?" Ricky scowls until Caleb looks away, although he's still grinning. Israfel half expects to be scowled at too, but the little smile is back in place when Ricky tips an imaginary hat in his direction. "All done, Padre. What'd you think?"

"You're wonderful," Israfel says, with absolute feeling. "You're all really *very* good. I'm impressed."

Ricky nods approval, as if this was all he had been waiting to hear. "Well, then. I'll see you tomorrow about the organ, Father. Come on, layabouts."

They file out. Israfel tests himself as they leave—"Goodnight, Sarah. Thanks, Mr. Hall."—until the door closes behind them and Israfel is left in the belfry alone.

With Nate.

Nate is apparently unfazed by this development. He's shifted position slightly over the course of the twenty minutes they've been standing here—his elbows are on the piano now, tucked in close to his sides so his hands dangle forward over the edge—but his chest and hips are still thrust forward, casual and devastating. Israfel wants to run his hands down Nate's smooth flanks through the thin fabric of his T-shirt, pull him close by his narrow hips.

Nate smirks, and for a moment of heart-stopping terror, Israfel is irrationally sure that Nate Mulligan can somehow read minds.

He says, because he has to say something, "So. Did you need something else, Nate?"

The smirk bleeds into something closer to a smile, and Israfel's heart quiets a little in his chest. Nate pushes himself up from the piano onto the balls of his feet and swings his arms as if to restore the circulation a little. Israfel chews the inside of his lip, berating himself. It isn't Nate's fault that he's perfect from every angle, that Israfel wants him in ways no man should want a seventeen-year-old boy. He needs to stop reading licentiousness into what Nate thinks of as comfortable positions.

"I came in to see if you were taking confession this evening, actually," Nate says, stretching his arms up above his head, easing his muscles. The gesture pulls his shirt away from the waistband of his jeans at one side, revealing a tiny sliver of flat stomach in the space between. "But you weren't, and it wasn't, you know, *urgent*. And I feel better now, so...." He shrugs and lifts up the other arm, entwining them over his head like vines. "It can wait till Sunday."

The T-shirt has crept up on both sides now, its hem clinging to Nate's stomach somewhere around the point of his navel. Below it are the outlines of muscles and a narrow trail of hair descending into his jeans.

Israfel clears his throat, thanks God sincerely for the skirt of his cassock, and says, "I thought you came in to hear the bells?"

Nate smiles. "I like the bells, sure, but I didn't come over here specially for that." He shrugs, lowering his arms at last. "But you were here, so...." The smile quirks a little, and Israfel's cheeks heat.

"I was here, so...?" he hears himself ask.

Nate shrugs. "I want to get to know you. It's only right, isn't it? We'll be seeing a lot of each other."

Israfel's pulse is rushing thickly in his wrists, at the pulse point in his neck. What Nate says is perfectly innocent, he knows, and perfectly true. There's neither sense nor need in getting worked up about it the way he's doing, and he swallows, willing himself calm. It isn't as if he's new to—he guesses—*crushes*, and he knows how to deal with them. When people don't crush back, there's only so long a fixation can survive.

And then Nate reaches over, his broad palm hovering an inch away from Israfel's sternum, his face suddenly close.

"I'll see you Sunday," he says, and his voice is bright and innocent, perfectly calm, as he draws two fingers lightly down Israfel's chest and over his stomach.

A moment later, Nate is gone, and so is Israfel's sense of everything he knows. The church is empty all around him, oppressive with age.

Israfel stares at the door for a long time while his mind fragments.

Four

THE parish committee meets on Friday evenings. As far as Israfel is concerned, it is this more than anything that distinguishes this church from the ones he's known before. Only the *extremely* involved churchgoer would regularly designate Friday evenings for sitting around the dining table in the draft-beset rectory discussing the fate of the church roof and other minor matters.

The committee is small, but very dedicated. Lynda Mulligan is the chairperson for the current term, and as such is seated at the head of the long table, directly opposite Israfel. Her youngest son has taken up residence on the armchair to Israfel's left, skinny legs swinging coltishly as he flips through a book. Lynda had been very apologetic—"I don't make a habit of bringing him along, Padre, but I had him in the car with me already, and I don't know if anyone is home right now."—but Israfel had waved her off with assurances that Tom was perfectly welcome, as indeed he is. The smile Israfel throws in his direction is, perhaps, mostly an expression of gratitude that he is the only Mulligan son currently present, but Tom doesn't need to know that. He smiles back anyway, and Israfel applies himself to his notes, feeling oddly reassured. Tom doesn't hate him. Nate evidently didn't go straight home and tell him tales of Israfel's untoward behavior, his obvious attentions in the belfry. For some reason, this lightens Israfel's heart, as if this possibility had been looming over his head, although he hasn't consciously thought of it before now.

The various motions are proposed and dealt with swiftly, or so it seems to Israfel. The committee works together with all the efficiency of long service, and he feels barely needed except to accept decisions already made. Afterward, there are tea and cookies on the sideboard, and Israfel feels a little lost. The committee is very tight, people who've lived and worked together for, in most cases, the greater part of their lives. Israfel suspects it will take him a while to feel part of the loop.

"Padre?" says a voice at his elbow.

Israfel turns, startled, passes a hand over his face. and smiles when he sees Tom. "Mmm?"

Tom smiles. "All right?"

"A little overwhelmed," Israfel admits with a sideways quirk of his mouth. "I have effectively *no* clue who most of these people are that they're all talking about, so...."

"Me either," Tom tells him confidentially. "Half the time, they're people who lived here thirty years ago. It's okay. You get used to it." He shrugs. "It's that kind of village."

"It's all old country up here," Israfel agrees and laughs shortly. "I'm sorry you had to sit through it. It can't be very interesting for you."

Tom grins ruefully. "Not really, no. But Nate's out with Alison Wright, and Mom for some reason thinks I can't be left in the house on my own." He pulls a face. "Which is *totally* dumb, since I'm thirteen years old."

"Alison Wright?"

The words are out before Israfel has had a chance to think about them, and he regrets them immediately. There is no reason on earth why Nate shouldn't go out with Alison Wright. She's a nice girl, as far as Israfel can tell, and certainly very attractive. But for some reason, he can't seem to let the comment go and move on by. It draws him like an itching sore or a road traffic accident. "Is she his girlfriend?" he asks, trying for casual and hoping he hasn't missed it by too great a distance.

Tom snorts. "Nate doesn't do girlfriends."

Israfel figures he must have pulled a rather odd expression, because Tom clarifies quickly, "Or I guess you could say he definitely does girlfriends, plural. He never goes out with the same girl twice." He wrinkles his nose. "He's like, addicted or something. And then he comes home and goes on and on about all the particular things that were great about every separate girl, and—" Tom breaks off, cheeks coloring a little. "I probably shouldn't be talking to you about this. Nate might actually kill me if he ends up in trouble."

Through the pounding of his pulse in his throat, Israfel manages to force out a laugh. He hopes it doesn't sound as awfully insincere as it feels. "He's not going to get in trouble from me, Tom. He's seventeen; these things happen. He actually came to me on Tuesday and said he wanted me to hear his confession; I guess this might have been why? In which case—" he spreads his hands "—he can make amends with God, as long as he's aware of his shortcomings. It's all right."

Tom's mouth twists. "Yeah, well. He couldn't make amends with Dad so easy." There's a thread coming loose where the pocket of his jeans joins the leg, and he picks at it distractedly. "Please don't... don't tell my mom I mentioned this, will you?"

"Promise," Israfel says, smiling. Inside, something is raking through his guts and churning them up into furrows, but the smile is reassuring.

Evidently, it works on Tom, who looks immediately relieved. "I never accidentally said stuff like this to our last priest," he confesses. "Father Zebadiah was about a million years old. And I think he was deaf." He studies Israfel for a moment, carefully. "But you're cool."

Israfel laughs and lays his palm gentle and brief against the top of Tom's head in the gesture of benediction. "Thank you, Tom."

Tom grins back, a little gap-toothed. "No problem."

"Tell your brother I said hello," says Israfel, because obviously his subconscious is a masochist.

Tom, oblivious of course, simply nods and says he will.

ON SUNDAY morning, Israfel puts on all his vestments in the rectory. He tells himself, as he arranges them over his shoulders, that there's no particular reason for this, and no particular reason why he shouldn't. But the pit of his stomach feels oddly hollow, apprehensive for reasons he has no wish to delve into, and a shiver trips down his spine as he smooths the fabric flat over his stomach. He has no wish to be seen without his armor, even the most superficial trappings of it. And if this is in defense against Nate, then at least Israfel will have made an attempt at personal protection.

As it happens, both boys are already in the sacristy when Israfel arrives, the very picture of youthful devotion in their surplices and good Sunday shoes. Israfel recalls, involuntarily, the pale strip of skin at Nate's waist, revealed by his long-armed stretch, his neat narrow hips in his jeans. Seeing him like this, every sinful line of him concealed beneath the white mantle, Israfel can barely collate the memory and the reality. That Nate, with his lounging, catlike grace, his slow smirks and intent touches—that Nate seems so far removed from this one that Israfel is almost sure, for a second heavy with guilt, that he only dreamed him out of lust.

Then Nate looks up and smiles at him, and the smile brings all the Nates together, even while it rends Israfel apart.

If it hadn't been for Tom, Israfel feels, they could have gone on looking at each other like that for moments upon moments, Israfel's own smile coaxed out of him by the sheer intensity in Nate's face, the draw of his wet dream of a mouth. But Tom is with them, and Israfel is relieved by the normality of his earnest, unbroken little voice, a reassurance that—incredibly—the sudden heat in the room is tangible only to Israfel.

"Morning, Father." Tom's grinning when Israfel manages to wrench his eyes from Nate, chest feeling oddly overfull with the combination of reluctance and relief. Tom's teeth are still too big for his mouth, and the little detail makes Israfel feel suddenly fond of him, in a reassuringly appropriate way.

"Morning, Tom. Nate." Israfel attempts to encompass them both in his smile, without really looking at either of them. He isn't very certain that it's working. Moreover, he has the most unsettling feeling that Nate has noticed his uncertainty, judging by the way his answering grin has begun to edge distinctly into smirking territory. Pointedly, Israfel clears his throat and turns toward the table. "Is everything ready?"

"Everything's ready," Nate shoots back, easy and slow, and Israfel curses him for his nonchalance, the low-pitched confidence in his voice that Israfel wants, horribly, to sink into as if it were warm water. "We were just waiting on your holiness to fix up the water."

Tom makes a little disapproving sound. "He's not a 'holiness', Nate. He's not the *Pope*."

Israfel bites his lip on a smile.

Nate shrugs expansively. "Well, whatever. He's still the only one here who can make this stuff Holy Water instead of just regular Evian, so there's got to be some kind of holiness in him, right?" He grins up at Israfel. "Right, Father?"

"He's just being a douche," Tom puts in hastily, through an expression of distaste that seems to be composed mostly of forehead. "You can ignore him when he gets like this; I always do."

"Nobody's being ignored," Israfel says, giving in to the impulse and letting himself laugh a little. "In answer to your question, Nate: I'm not 'holy'"—he makes little quotation marks around the word with his fingers—"in and of myself, but I'm an anointed representative of Christ, so I can invest *His* holiness into the water. That's all." He shrugs.

Nate considers this for a minute, eyebrows drawing together in the middle. He looks ridiculous and adorable, and Israfel is content to watch him think.

At length, he says, "So... you're saying you're like, God's realtor? And you have the keys to all his properties or something?"

Israfel laughs and raises his eyebrows approvingly. "Not a bad analogy, actually. The Lord's servants keep the keys to His Kingdom, after all, don't we?"

The look on Tom's face says quite clearly that he's struggling between a certain quiet pleasure in the aptness of the equation and disgruntlement that Nate had thrown it out so flippantly and been commended for it. Israfel reaches out and touches his forehead, tells him, to soothe the waters, "But you were quite right, Tom. A priest has no inherent holiness of his own."

When he pulls back, Tom looks altogether more contented, but Nate is arching an eyebrow at him, mouth drawn together pointedly into something dangerously close to a pout. Israfel laughs and shrugs a little. "Something wrong, Nate?"

"He got extra blessings!" Nate manages to invest his voice with a convincing amount of outrage, despite the throaty undertone to it that suggests a root in amusement rather than genuine indignation. "When I was right!" He frowns at Israfel. "If I get rollered by a truck on the way out of here today, Padre, you're gonna feel real guilty." He lifts his head. "Come on, I want an extra holy hit, too."

Tom is rolling his eyes exaggeratedly, but Israfel, despite his better judgment, can't help but be amused. Nate's face is upturned to his, appealing, and his hair looks so *soft*. Israfel's hand is hovering over his forehead before he can stop himself. "Fine. But I'll have you know that you've guilted me into this one. I can't guarantee that it'll be worth as much." His palm settles lightly against Nate's forehead, the tips of his fingers just resting, traitorous, in Nate's hair.

Nate smiles up at him, warm and close, and somehow—Israfel could swear to it—a little smug. "Nah, I trust you, Father. I bet you always do it right."

He throws the words out casually, but that low pitch to his voice has returned, that particular brightness in his eyes. Israfel swallows and draws his hand firmly away. "You're not going to get hit by any cars," he says irrelevantly, for the sake of something to say, something to move things out of the strange, crackling quietude between them.

"Yeah, Nate," Tom says. "I forbid you to be hit by a car."

Nate shrugs. "Father Raf is gonna bless me again after he's taken my confession, anyway, so I should be good." He glances up at Israfel. "Aren't you?"

The confession had slipped Israfel's mind—although now, he cannot understand how he could have forgotten about it. Listening to Nate confess his various transgressions with the less-dedicated girls in the village is not something he much looks forward to. Still, perhaps it will be good for him, bring home to him the ludicrousness of his feelings, his occasional deluded convictions about Nate's own behavior.

"Of course," he assures, reaching for the water. "Of course."

Five

IN LARGER churches, where the congregation allows, a priest usually has three altar servers to help him: Candle, Cross, and Book. Here, the servers work only in two-person teams, with the result that one server is left with the dual responsibility of carrying the candles and holding the missal for the priest while he reads the Hours. Nate, being the tallest by a considerable amount, habitually carries the cross. Ostensibly, this is so that the cross will be visible to everyone. In fact, Israfel suspects, Nate is always Cross because it means he can then sit down for long periods, instead of having to stand still and serve as a sort of human lectern.

Sunday services are always particularly long, and by the end, Tom is wilting. Israfel smiles at him sympathetically as he takes the missal from him, noting the trembling of his arms.

"All done, Tom," he says. "You can go home now and give your arms a rest. Unless you're staying for confession?"

"He should be," Nate puts in breezily, wandering over with the candles. "He needs to do penance for the fact that he's spent the past thirty minutes cursing everything and promising his kingdom for a chair—ain't that right, Tommy?"

Both hands being occupied, Nate is reduced to nudging his brother with his hip. It makes contact somewhere close to Tom's elbow, which Israfel finds simultaneously adorable and pitiful. But then, Tom should be hitting his growth spurt any time now.

"No thanks to you," Tom retorts grumpily. "I'm not staying for confession. I have homework to do, and I've been good, unlike some people." He prods Nate in the small of the back, nudging him toward the sacristy. "You better be confessing to making your brother carry the world's most enormous book, *again.*"

"I had to carry the cross!" Nate protests, letting himself be nudged. "That's way heavier! C'mon, Tom; I am an *awesome* brother."

"You had to carry the cross for, like, a minute, Nate. And you suck." Tom looks up at Israfel. "Father, next time it's our turn, can I be Cross?"

Israfel smiles, hefting the missal under his arm. It really is heavy. "Of course. I think it's probably time you two started taking turns, hmm?"

Now safely within the confines of the sacristy, Nate shrugs and pulls his surplice up and over his head. His T-shirt comes most of the way up with it, and Israfel feels his face growing hot.

"Fine," Nate says, muffled through the folds of surplice and shirt, "but we rotate, okay?"

The end of "okay" breaks suddenly clear as Nate's head emerges from the bundle of white cloth, his hair sticking up wildly at one side. Tom snorts, stretching up on his toes to smooth down the impromptu quiff, and Israfel bites back another entirely ridiculous surge of envy.

"Sure, Nate," Tom says, and Israfel can hear that he's mollified, despite the skeptical tone to his voice. He takes off his own surplice carefully, folding it and setting it aside. Exactly no amount of T-shirt comes up with it, and Israfel is uncomfortably sure that no amount of T-shirt normally *would*, unless it was intended to.

"See you later, then. Mom and Dad aren't staying after, so you'll have to walk."

"I'm sure I can manage, squirt," Nate says, hefting himself up onto the table. He reaches out with a toe, shoving at Tom's skinny thigh. "Go on; get. See you later."

"You better confess being mean to me!" Tom throws over his shoulder as he leaves.

Nate rolls his eyes and looks at Israfel, and here he is again, alone with Nate in a small and silent room. Israfel's collar is suddenly uncomfortably tight, and he tugs at it a little nervously.

"Well," he says, "I, uh. I should be getting down to the confessional; I'm running late. I suppose I'll see you there." Self-consciously, he reaches up to adjust the hang of his vestments over his shoulders.

"Don't worry, Padre; you look great." Nate smiles up at him, feet swinging indolent and self-assured. Israfel raises his eyebrows a little, but Nate just goes on smiling. "Go on, listen to everyone's dastardly deeds, huh? I'll catch you later."

Israfel, fumbling for the last of his dignity, lifts his chin and smiles. His stomach is once again churning like a cement mixer, but he hopes he looks composed. "All right, Nate. You'll know where to find me when you're ready."

He turns before Nate can say anything else and strides out of the sacristy, but as he walks, he could swear that he can hear Nate's soft laughter behind him.

Dastardly deeds are, it seems, rather few and far between in this village. It isn't that Israfel *wants* to find himself in the uncomfortable position of hearing a confession of murder, but confessions of covetousness directed toward other people's shoes and interior decoration swiftly become mind-numbingly dull. As a means of distracting himself, he concentrates on identifying voices, matching them to faces, and then struggling to apply the correct names. The first two women he knows already, having seen them lined up outside the booth, so that's something of a cheat. The next three, and one man, must have arrived at some point during the first confession, so Israfel thinks hard on those. The man he knows is Mr. (Alexander) Barton. Two of the women he can guess at. The other eludes him. There's a grille, of course, separating the two halves of the booth, but it's rather fine-milled, and very little is visible.

After the nameless woman, he hears a male voice upon which he doesn't have to think at *all*.

"In the name of the Father," Nate says, low and soft, "and of the Son, and of the Holy Spirit. My last confession was five weeks ago."

Israfel's heart seems to rise up thick in his throat, pulse beating heavy in the hollows. "May the Lord bless and keep you, my son," he says. "Do you have sins you wish to confess today?"

Nate breathes in and then out again, a deep, soft sigh. The point of the confessional is to engender an intimacy, a place of safety for priest and penitent together, but Israfel feels anything but safe like this. He can hear Nate breathe, hear the shifting of his clothes when he moves. In the darkness, Israfel's awareness of Nate's body is still more acute, and the prickling of his spine is unnerving.

At length, Nate says, "Yes, Father. I have sinned."

Israfel waits. Sometimes, priests will punctuate penitents' confessions with prayers, but Israfel prefers to prompt only when necessary. Most of his penitents today have hesitated a little, from which Israfel deduces that his forerunner was more of a prompting sort. But, like those who came before him, Nate recognizes after a minute that it is still his turn to speak.

"I, uh." He clears his throat. "I've given myself in sexual gratification." A pause. "Um, a lot."

The skin on Israfel's cheeks feels uncomfortably tight. He finds himself nodding before he remembers that Nate can't see. "Go on."

"Well," Nate says, "three separate girls gave me head in the back of my car." There's a sound which Israfel charitably hopes is a cough. "One of 'em five different times, and this chick has an *incredible* talent."

Israfel frowns a little. Nate has been giving confession, surely, for many years already. He can't imagine that he's unaware that "go on" means "and the next sin, please" and not "please expand in detail upon the sin already noted." But then, possibly Father Zebadiah just sat there and said "next sin," or something equally impossible to misinterpret.

Possibly.

He can give Nate the benefit of the doubt.

"All right. You're aware that sex outside of marriage is an offense in the eyes of God?"

A sigh from Nate. "Yes."

"And you are aware that this is particularly true of sexual acts not oriented toward procreation?"

Nate shifts a little, the roughness of denim scraping against the chair. "Yes, Father, I am aware."

"All right," says Israfel, folding his hands in his lap. "Next sin."

"Well," Nate says, "that last girl. I fucked her." He shifts again, rasp of denim against the hardwood chair, and Israfel shifts too, battling back the fragmentary images trying to birth themselves in the unwatched part of his mind.

"Oh, and I was wearing a condom," Nate adds, "which I guess makes everything worse, huh?" He laughs shortly, and this time Israfel can't even begin to pretend that it's a cough. "Shame, really. I bet she would've felt better without, all hot and wet and skin on skin." Another laugh. "*And* it woulda been less sinful. But I guess she'd have liked me a lot less if I'd gotten her pregnant, so…. You win some, you lose some, right?"

Israfel's voice is strained when it emerges, a little roughened, lower pitched than usual. He sincerely hopes that Nate doesn't notice, but something tells him Nate already has. "It doesn't quite work like that, my son. Extramarital sex of any kind is a mortal sin. The use of prophylactics is a venial sin when it occurs within marriage; in the context of extramarital sex, the detail isn't terribly relevant."

"Oh," Nate says. Just that, just, "Oh," and the tone of his voice sparks a heat in Israfel's gut, sends it rolling in waves through his pelvis.

Israfel is evidently doomed.

Then Nate says, contemplatively, "So all extramarital sex is pretty much equal, then, right?"

Israfel furrows his brow, wondering if all Nate's confessions are going to be along these lines. The Confessional is not ordinarily used to give guidance upon the interpretation of Church Law. "In general, yes. Extramarital sex with a married woman is a graver sin, but I hope you haven't been guilty of that." The "Nate" on the end is only just bitten back in Israfel's mouth. This is supposed to be anonymous, he reminds himself, supposed to be absolution. The fact that it's beginning to feel like some kind of dirty drinking game doesn't mean he can break the rules of the Confessional.

The rules of the Confessional are sacred.

Nate laughs softly, a little huff of breath. "Not that one, no." He pauses. "But, Father... I've been having these... thoughts."

Israfel says nothing. His throat feels as if it's been stuffed up with cotton wool, so speaking would be rather difficult. Hopefully, Nate will remember himself and continue.

"Impure thoughts," Nate clarifies. "I mean, I wasn't looking at porn or nothing, just...." He trails off. His breathing is coming faster now, and suddenly closer, as if he's leaned toward the grille. "There's just this guy, Father."

A spike of sensation lances Israfel through, all guilt and want and disbelief, and he shifts nervously on the chair, easing the swell between his legs. "Go on," he manages, voice barely above a whisper.

"He's really hot," Nate says, mouth held near to the grille so his words are soft and close. "He's got this really *grabbable* hair, y'know? And every time I see him, it's like… I keep thinking about fisting my hands in it, pulling him in for a kiss."

Israfel's breathing is growing labored, but he's powerless to stop it, powerless, too, to say anything, to stop this before it ruins him entirely. It will be all right, he tells himself, clenching his fists on his thighs. Probably, Nate is fixated on another boy. Israfel knows exactly how difficult that can be. Nate will confess, and Israfel will give him penance and absolution, and this will be the last he ever hears of this.

He hasn't the composure to say "Go on," but Nate continues anyway.

"And his *mouth*, Father. I think it's the mouth that started it— that and his eyes." He swallows, audible and thick in his throat. "It just looks so fu—so incredibly soft, I can't stop thinking about it." A hitch of his breath. "I think about what it would feel like to fuck it, Father. That's what I was thinking about when that chick was blowing me in my car."

The whimper that breaks from Israfel's lips is a betrayal, a reflex of his body that his mind cannot forgive. He closes his eyes, as if that can drag the soft sound back again, but it's too late. Nate must have heard. Israfel swallows hard, reaches to his throat for his rosary. "Homosexual behavior is a grave sin," he manages, and it feels like the greatest achievement of his life that the words are almost level, although his voice is breaking.

"I know," says Nate, in this fine-threaded whisper of a voice. Israfel feels himself twitch distinctly beneath the cassock and tightens his fingers in shame around his crucifix.

"But I haven't," Nate is saying, and then there's a *snick* and a rustling of cloth, of skin. "Haven't *done* anything... uh...." And the soft sound shoots straight to Israfel's groin: a breathy groan and then the pull of skin against skin.

Oh, Israfel has to stop this. *Now.*

"My son," he rasps out, "Let me... let me absolve you."

It's too soon, he knows, a rush of a confession, throwing due ceremony to the winds. But that soft sound is the drag of Nate's palm on his cock, and Israfel can't listen to this and live.

"*Nnngh.*" Nate's shifting on the chair now, angling into his hand, and Israfel feels like his lip will split any second, purely from the desperate press of his teeth. "God, I fucking need absolution, Father. Think about... about going to my knees for him, lifting up his stupid fucking cassock and sucking his cock."

"Oh... God...," Israfel says, involuntarily, and it's three-quarters a prayer.

Nate's hand is moving faster now, the smell of him earthy and strong in the closeness of the booth. There's a slickness audible under the pulls, the slickness of *Nate* and he's thinking of....

"Father," Nate pants, "I know you want it... *Christ*... want to fuck my mouth, feel me taking you in... *fuck*, Israfel—"

And then his voice is breaking, shattering into gasps and a rough, choked-off moan, and Israfel is speechless, stunned, his whole world dissolving around him. For what seems like forever, there's nothing but the sound of Nate's breathing as it slows, eventually, the sound of his zipper being fastened.

Israfel's cheeks are burning, his temples damp with sweat. The pounding of his sin between his legs is a physical pain. At length, he says, because he can say nothing else, "Absolution?"

"I'm not sorry," Nate says, in a voice rough with sex and conviction.

Israfel blinks, tightens his fist around the crucifix, and swallows. "My son?"

"I'm not sorry I want you," Nate says again, with a forthrightness that makes Israfel shudder. "I don't want to be absolved of it, Father."

And then, suddenly, there is light and a rush of air. The door to Nate's side of the booth is open. Israfel, startled, leaps to his feet, cries out, "Nate!" through the grille, forgetting himself.

"Yeah," Nate says, low and soft and smiling. "See you soon, Father."

The door bangs closed again, throwing Israfel into darkness. The confessional reeks of sex and sin, and the next person to enter can't possibly fail to notice it. Israfel is blank, his rosary cradled in his palm.

"Hail Mary, full of grace," he begins, fingering the first bead on the string. "Our Lord is with thee. Blessed art thou amongst women...."

He prays like this, desperately, for perhaps a minute, perhaps two, perhaps five. Nobody pushes at the door of the booth. The church is empty and silent beyond this little space, beyond the turmoil in Israfel's mind.

He could leave now, he knows, get out and go home to the rectory, take off his vestments and go about his business. But it is safe here without Nate in the other booth. He is safe with his prayers and his beads and his garments of God. He brings the crucifix to his lips and holds it there, whispering the words against it, as if perhaps God will hear them better through the silver of the cross.

"Hail Mary, full of grace. Our Lord is with thee. Blessed art thou among women, and blessed is the fruit of thy womb, Jesus. Holy Mary, Mother of God, pray for us sinners, now and at the hour of our death. Amen."

Six

ONE of the advantages to presiding over an unusually busy parish is that there is rarely, as there might be elsewhere, a great deal of time left to oneself. In the hours following the Sunday morning service, Israfel's mind is nothing but chaos, apprehension, and distress bleeding into guilt and, occasionally, flashes of hope, swiftly quashed. Until dinnertime, Israfel makes no great attempt to wrest himself out of this cycle of mental tumult interspersed with prayer, the last hope of the desperate man.

But after dinner comes evening, and after evening, sleep, and then Israfel will find himself facing an early Latin Mass, unprepared. Israfel is nothing if not diligent. His career has been made, quite literally, through his capacity to put the Church before himself. And so he withdraws, with a great effort, from the circular paths he has trodden and re-trodden into grooves in his mind and sets himself to the task of reading over the Mass and locating the appropriate Bible passages. At first, of course, it is difficult—monumentally difficult, now that his brain knows the sound of Nate's climax and the blood rush of guilt that always accompanies the memory—but Israfel has always found Latin soothing, has always been able to lose himself in its cadences and cases. Having once hooked himself into the text, he manages to wade through it without too great a loss of concentration, and the Mass the following morning, although delivered after a night of rather broken sleep, goes as smoothly as any he's given before.

After the first time, things are easier. Israfel knows that, having successfully distracted himself once, he can do so again, can simply pour himself wholesale into any and every task that might require his attention and smother thoughts of Nate whenever they arise. The session in the confessional is something so entirely alien to Israfel's experience, so patently wrong and violently troubling, that Israfel cannot even begin to process or explain it, and furthermore, he is assured that no good could ever come from getting to the bottom of it. As such, the only thing to do is to ignore it, bury it under coffee mornings and homily writing and devotion, and pray to the Lord that he will perform some sort of minor miracle and erase Nate's memory of the event altogether.

Israfel holds out no great hope for his miracle, but it's always worth a prayer or two.

By Thursday morning, Israfel has settled rather well into his routine of denial, prayer, and distracting hyperactivity. He would not ordinarily be called upon to play any particular role in the monthly bake sale, but this week, Israfel does everything. The opportunity to fill up not only a morning with a social gathering, but also the preceding evening with throwing together a few basic cakes, was more than welcome.

Looking at his own offerings now, on a long table stacked with baked goods from the hands of hardy bakers whose proficiency in the kitchen has reached a level of artistry, he is forced to admit they look a little pitiful. Still, he suspects that a priest who can bake a cake, however simplistic, will strike at least somebody as novel enough that the idea of parting with a dollar or two for the product might not be too great a hardship.

Israfel is in the parish hall at eight thirty putting cloths on tables and generally allowing himself to be ordered around by elderly female pillars of the community, although the sale itself doesn't open until nine. Other people, Israfel swiftly discovers, are less scrupulous about such minor details as stated opening times. New cakes appear on the table with astonishing regularity as people arrive—some ten minutes late, and then thirty, and then fifty—and add their donations to the collection. When Israfel remarks upon this—casually, and, he hopes, without sounding condemnatory—to Mrs. Miller, he only gets a laugh and a dismissive wave of her wrinkled hand.

"Oh, that's just the way we do it around here, Father. Some folks take in all the donations the night before and set them all out in time for opening, but we've never been that way. Rotating stock, that's what it is. People come and go as they like and bring whatever they're bringing." She shrugs. "We're less likely to end up with a lot of squashed cakes, I can tell you that much. Isn't that so, Lynda?"

Israfel experiences a moment of extreme confusion before his mind clues in to the fact that Mrs. Miller is, quite evidently, no longer speaking to him. Glancing over his shoulder, he is, shamefully, rather disappointed—although not surprised—to see Lynda Mulligan, a large wrapped cake cradled in her arms.

"Hmm?" Lynda flashes a smile at Mrs. Miller and begins scrutinizing the table for an empty space. "What was that, Sarah?"

"I was just telling the Father here about our rotating stock," Mrs. Miller explains. "Folk just bring things as and when at our bake sales, don't they?"

"That's true enough," Lynda admits, nudging aside a few stray cupcakes in order to set her cake, on its enormous platter, down on the table. "There wouldn't have been space for this leviathan before, would there?" She indicates the cake and laughs. "And there's more where that came from. Nate is just coming with the cookies."

Israfel is in the process of collecting up empty plates into a stack cradled in the crook of his arm when the word "Nate" passes

Lynda's lips. The plates clink together alarmingly at his involuntary jerk. "You brought Nate with you?"

"Of course!" If Lynda has noticed his slip, she says nothing about it. Israfel prays briefly and fervently to God that his alarm went genuinely unremarked. "I need a big, strong man to cart my produce around, don't I, baby?"

"Sure do," Nate agrees, ducking out of the thickening crowd and under his mother's outstretched arm. There's a plate in his hand and another cradled in the crook of his elbow. In his other hand is a brown paper bag, whose contents Israfel cannot even begin to guess at. He looks ludicrously, criminally attractive in a moss-green shirt, and although he's leaning into Lynda, he's looking directly at Israfel. The sideways quirk of his smile, Israfel thinks hopelessly, could have rendered Samson kitten-weak with want.

"Plates!" Israfel announces, a note of desperation coloring his voice. One glance is enough to tell him that this *has* struck both Mrs. Miller and Mrs. Mulligan as a little odd, so Israfel swallows hard and tries to steady himself.

"We have too many empty plates," he clarifies, struggling not to shift his feet while every fiber in his body is tensed for flight. "And since Nate's been kind enough to carry all these things for you"—Israfel studiously avoids Nate's eye—"it might be nice if he had somewhere to put them, mightn't it? So...." He indicates the stack of plates in his arms, clutches it to his chest protectively. "I'll just... get rid of these. If you'll excuse me, ladies."

Israfel's retreat to the kitchen is not his most dignified moment, but as Israfel sees it, it's nothing to the beating his dignity might have taken if he'd stood there any longer, letting Nate look at him, all cocky and perfect. *Why* Nate would come here, knowing Israfel would be here, he can hardly begin to fathom. The only logical explanation seems to be that he came at his mother's bidding, presumably under the impression that Israfel would have avoided bake sales as his predecessor had done—and as, indeed, most priests would. If this is true, then Nate is probably as embarrassed to see Israfel as Israfel is to see him, or even if he hasn't exactly shown any sign of embarrassment, he'll still be surprised that Israfel is here. There is nothing Nate could possibly have to say to him, Israfel thinks. This is all a misunderstanding, and his speedy retreat to the kitchen is probably the best thing he could have done for either of them.

He's leaning back against the counter, eyes closed and breathing deeply, when he hears Nate say, "Need a hand?"

Nate is young and light-footed, for sure, but still, Israfel is a little unnerved by how quietly he moves, how far into the room he has advanced, unnoticed. Israfel opens his eyes immediately, a guilty flush creeping over his cheekbones, to find Nate almost at his elbow, three empty plates in the crook of one arm, the same little smirk still playing about his lips.

"Nate," he begins, and then falters because there is simply nothing else he knows how to say. Referring to the incident would seem foolhardy, at best. Behaving as if it had never happened is not something he is certain he can achieve, not with Nate so close—and so unrepentant.

Nate only grins a little more at Israfel's hesitance, leans past him to set down the plates on the counter. The movement puts him still closer to Israfel, his nose almost brushing Israfel's cheek as he starts to lean away again, and Israfel is near trembling at the proximity, knuckles whitening on the edge of the countertop.

He makes no sound; of this, he is fairly certain. But even so, Nate does not draw away as Israfel prays he will. Instead, he only turns his face so his lips brush the nautilus of Israfel's ear, so the heat of his breath ghosts down the exposed column of his neck.

"Aren't you happy to see me?"

He's half laughing, voice rich as cream with it. Israfel breathes in shortly and turns his face away. "Nate, I'm busy," he says as steadily as he can manage, although his cheeks are burning and his game is up.

"Right." Nate's fingers curl around his jaw, then, turn him easily, casually back until their eyes meet. "I can see you're real busy out here." His tongue darts out, leaving a shimmer on his lower lip, and then, incredibly, he leans forward.

Israfel, desperate, closes his eyes in the only act of self-preservation left to him. "Nate, *please.*"

Nate laughs, warm exhalation against Israfel's lips. "You don't have to plead with me, Father." And then there's an unfamiliar softness, a dry warmth against Israfel's mouth that dampens when Nate's lips part and catch at the swell of Israfel's lower lip.

"Nate!"

It is shock more than anything else that brings Israfel's hands to Nate's shoulders to shove him a half step backwards. Seeing him like this, his eyes washed dark, pupils bleeding out into the green, Israfel isn't sure he could ever have rejected him without the adrenal element of shock at his back, and that is a terrifying thought. "Nate, *no.*"

Nate's hands haven't moved, one still curled around Israfel's jaw while the other, Israfel notes with a jolt of fear-want-*no*, has come to rest at his waist. He looks anything but terrified.

"No?" He leans in again—slowly at first—and then, as if assured that Israfel isn't about to shove him away again, brushes his open mouth against Israfel's closed one. "Really?" His thumb swipes a smooth stroke over Israfel's jawbone, setting the nerve endings alight with energy. He presses a kiss to one corner of Israfel's mouth, then slightly further toward the center, and Israfel is incapable of stopping him. Everything in him yearns to give in to the touch, to pull Nate against him and open his mouth and drink him in.

It's *wrong.* Oh, it's *so* wrong. It's the wrongest thing Israfel has ever done, and he is under no illusions about it. It would be wrong for any God-fearing man to let himself be touched like this. For Israfel to allow it is a blasphemy, just as he is a blasphemy of a man, subverted and cursed. He struggles for enough breath to make a last attempt, but even the brush of his mouth opening against Nate's seems to seize him up inside, whispering of his certain damnation.

"Nate, why? Why are you doing this?"

"You want me to," Nate whispers, simple and assured.

And Israfel, God save him, does. There is nothing else he can say.

The next push of Nate's mouth is surer, more insistent, and Israfel can offer no resistance. It has been years since Israfel has been kissed like this, and he has no doubt that he is clumsy, but Nate doesn't seem to mind. He works Israfel's mouth deftly open with his own, sucking on his upper lip until Israfel gasps for air, and then descending expertly to trace his tongue along the lower ridge of his teeth. The multitude of sensations leaves Israfel dizzy, almost drunk, makes him fist his hands in Nate's shirt half unconsciously as he works his mouth slowly against Nate's. The voice in the back of his mind—the voice that keeps Israfel together; what he likes to think of as his conscience—is screaming, but Israfel's skin is screaming, too, and what it wants is *Nate*. Nate's mouth is clever and quick, tongue flickering against Israfel's lips, and it shreds Israfel like so much flimsy paper.

If things could simply continue like this forever, Israfel feels, he would not be able to protest. Not with Nate's body pressed warm to his, Nate's hand firm on his face. The touch of his mouth is magic, and Israfel is ensnared by it. But there are other snares on Israfel too, and when Nate's hand trips lower, the heel of it pressing against the swell below Israfel's belt, their teeth snap through him, sudden and vicious, make him tear his mouth away and seize Nate's wrist.

"Nate," Israfel says. He feels as if he's said it a lot, today: *Nate, don't. Nate, no. Nate, please.* But it is the only thing in his mind, after all: this endless repetition of *natenatenatenate* that seems to thunder through him with his pulse. "Please. I can't...." He reaches up, pressing a hand to his face, and shakes his head helplessly. "I just... I *can't*." His breath is coming quick and shallow, and he knows it, but he must push on. "Perhaps I do… want you. That doesn't mean we can do this, Nate. One of these days I might feel like killing someone; it doesn't mean I can just go ahead and do it."

A little fortified, he pushes Nate carefully away, takes a step sideways. "We have to control ourselves, all right? Of course we're all human, but we're not animals. Control is what righteousness *is*."

His voice is breaking over the words, fragmenting with effort, but Nate is just… looking at him, just standing there with his hands by his sides, jeans tented visibly at the crotch, and *looking*.

"Nate," Israfel says again, when he can't stand it any longer. "Nate, do you understand?"

There's another tortuous beat of silence. Then Nate shakes his head, slow and almost disappointed. "I don't think *you* understand, Father," he says, after a moment. "You're so fucking clever, but you don't know anything about anything, do you?"

Israfel opens his mouth. Nate gives him a minute, crossing his arms as he waits, but Israfel is empty, a void. He has nothing to say. He knows nothing, and after a pause, Nate shakes his head again, turns on his heel and leaves, footsteps silent on the polished wooden floor.

Israfel, left alone in the kitchen with a stack of empty plates and a far larger stack of questions, can't help feeling that Nate is right. In this moment, he feels as if he has never known anything about anything at all.

Seven

NATE'S mouth tastes of coffee, bitter and sweet. The wind is up, a white October wind, but Israfel feels no chill with Nate in his arms, Nate, who seems to radiate warmth. More than warmth, even. It's dark, and Israfel's feet are bare in the damp grass, but there's a light in Nate that draws Israfel to him, more surely than the light of noon, and it glows still, makes for them a circle of security, an island in the dead of the night.

Nate doesn't speak. Israfel does not expect him to. His clothes seem to melt from his body the instant Israfel touches them, like ice burnt away by the fire of his devotion. Nate's skin, revealed to Israfel's sight, is everywhere illuminated. Under Israfel's mouth, it runs as smooth and pure as silk or cream, and his hair is thick and soft between Israfel's fingers. Israfel cannot be still, must know him everywhere: the spur of his hip; his dark, peaked nipples; the buttered sharpness of his clavicle against the rough of Israfel's tongue. What sounds fall from his lips are inchoate, meaningless, but Israfel kisses prayers into his skin, opens Nate up easy as breathing, and it's perfect, the inside of Nate a haven for Israfel, a safe harbor in which he moors.

The next thing Israfel sees is a lemon-yellow sheet. One moment he's sliding reverentially into Nate on some dark hillside, and the next there's a lemon-yellow sheet, but that's the way things roll. Israfel isn't terribly bothered by it.

Nate, it seems, is more so, or at least, he's no longer content to be made love to slow and quiet. Israfel's on his back before he's fully processed where they are, and then there is Nate rising naked above him—slim, muscled thighs spread astride Israfel's hips—against the yellow wallpaper of the bedroom Israfel grew up in.

Israfel remains unsurprised, but possibly that has something to do with the way Nate is rolling his hips, leaning back against Israfel's raised knees, spine arched, long throat exposed and vulnerable. His cock is hard and insistent, smearing slickness over his stomach as he moves, and Israfel reaches for it, rubs his thumb over the tip and rocks his pelvis up at Nate's groan of approval. His feet are flat to the bed, toes curling for purchase, and the fingers of his left hand are bruisingly tight on Nate's hip, holding him still.

It's evident just from the sight of him that Nate is close. The way he fucks himself punishingly on Israfel's cock, his movements becoming erratic with desperation, and the litany of curses and demands he wrenches out as he moves: "Fuck me... " and "Shit, like that... " and "Jesus fucking Christ, don't *stop*." Israfel grits his teeth against the steady build of pressure in his abdomen, works his fist furiously on Nate as he picks up speed. He's close, too, so fucking close, vision whiting out at the edges, but Nate's not done, torquing and crying out and rocking sweat slick against Israfel, and so he only holds onto himself and fucks until Nate's body arches and stills, come pulsing out of him like triumph.

"Nate," Israfel manages, "God, Nate, you're so, you're *so*... I *can't*...."

And then there is stickiness all over Israfel's belly. Which would be all right, were it not for the fact that the stickiness has also spread to his pajama bottoms, the T-shirt he sleeps in, and the sheets. Which, for the record, are pale blue and do not play host to anyone but Israfel.

Israfel clenches his fist in frustration and shame and presses his face into his pillow. To add insult to injury, he swiftly discovers that even it has not escaped unscathed, jerking upright when his cheek comes into contact with the cooling puddle of drool on the pillowcase.

"Shit," he says aloud, scrubbing his hands over his eyes.

Israfel's not much given to swearing, but *fuck*, he feels as if he has good reason.

Eight

ISRAFEL VACEK was eleven years old when he first began to feel he wasn't "right."

For most boys, the process of realization would have been delayed by another couple of years at least, but most boys have nobody against whom to really compare themselves, nobody to use as a yardstick in their journey toward normal adulthood. Israfel, on the other hand, was the younger, by fourteen minutes, of monozygotic twins, and had been used to direct comparison all his life.

Nobody was ever in very much doubt about the fact that Michael was his superior, both preferable and preferred.

Physically, of course, they were identical. Academically, also, they were well matched, challenged in class only by each other. This, though, was where the similarities ended.

In their elementary school years, the two of them had never socialized much with outsiders, preferring to sit together in class and confuse their teachers. They had played together at recess, studied together after school, and stood together in the church choir on Sundays and during Wednesday rehearsal. Israfel had always been possessed of a rampant and fertile imagination, which Michael delighted in and encouraged. At night, from his upper bunk, Israfel would tell stories of the Otherworld, where everything was upside down and the Vacek brothers were heroes. Underneath him in the dark, Michael would encourage and advise, creating monsters and dragons and knights for Israfel to weave into his plot. The two of them were, Mrs. Vacek liked to say, a perfect matched set. Her clever, handsome boys, made to be each other's best friend, and for a long time, it was true.

Then, when they were eleven, the unimaginable happened. Mr. Vacek came home one day from the office with a flier in his hand, which he presented to his sons with a flourish. "Found this on the notice board, boys. Interested?"

They squinted at it together. It called for boys between ten and thirteen to try out for a local baseball team that needed numbers. Israfel, entirely disinterested, shrugged and shook his head. "I'm not much for baseball," he said, moving to return the flier to his father.

"Hey." Michael smiled at him sidelong, but his grip on the flier was viselike, holding it still. "I'll give it a shot, Dad," he said, grinning up at Mr. Vacek.

As moments go, Israfel supposes it shouldn't have been so monumental. He doubts that Michael would remember the scene at all, if he were to bring it up. But to Israfel, this was, in every way, a first. This was the first time Michael had disagreed with him about an activity, the first time Israfel had ever been made to realize that the two of them might differ in their likes and dislikes. It was the first time, also, that he'd felt his father's favor shine on Michael without ever touching him. More importantly, perhaps, it was the first time he'd ever felt *wrong* for not wanting to do something a parent had suggested, the first time he'd felt his desires veer from the black centerline of "normal."

For Michael, probably, that baseball group was only his first sports team. For Israfel, it marked the beginning of the end.

That was where the deviation began—slowly, at first—with Michael making outside friends at baseball whose names he would mention breezily to Israfel in casual conversation. Soon enough, though, Michael began to venture out with his baseball friends on Saturday afternoons, and a little after that, Israfel noticed that Michael was making friends at school too. One morning, he walked into the classroom to find that Michael had sat down next to Gabriel Constant and was unconcernedly unpacking his satchel onto the desk.

Neither of them said anything, but it didn't really feel as if they had to.

By the time they were fourteen, they had established separate social circles which barely even overlapped at the edges. Michael's was vast, encompassing the school athletes and the pretty girls who waved pompoms on the sidelines. Israfel's, on the other hand, comprised only two or three other boys, all as quiet and scholarly as he was himself. At night, Israfel still told his stories of Otherworld, and Michael still laughed and contributed and played along, but it went without saying that this wasn't to be mentioned during the day, that Michael was a little ashamed of enjoying his brother's company. Somewhere along the way, Michael had entered the arena of the popular kids, while Israfel hung out with the budding poets and mathletes. The differences were not as stark as they would have been in a cutthroat public school—they were all, at least, united by the blandness of the Catholic school uniform—but nevertheless, they were there, and they were felt. Israfel's friends were nice kids, but he missed Michael the way he'd been when they were ten, when they were each other's whole world. He lived for the nighttime, for that universe in the darkness behind their eyelids where they had each other's backs, where they conquered and soared together.

When Michael was fifteen, he acquired his first girlfriend. Mrs. Vacek pretended, briefly, to be concerned about this, but then they had her over to dinner and she fell head over heels for Alice's blonde braids and fresh-faced, unthreatening smile. Michael was obsessed with her, and Mr. Vacek made no attempt to conceal his pride at the development.

Israfel had no particular dislike for Alice, but the whole thing made him want to die.

The thing was, it wasn't as if Israfel couldn't have had his own choice of girls, if he'd had the inclination. He was shy and studious, but some people liked that. Israfel knew that people thought Michael attractive, and objectively, this must mean they'd find him equally so. But he had no close female friends, and he couldn't even imagine pursuing an intimate relationship, however innocent, with someone he wasn't already attached to. He knew Michael was content to believe that his brother simply hadn't "developed" yet, but this wasn't exactly true.

For two years, he had been waking, sticky and shamefaced, from vague, unsettling dreams. Probably, he could have avoided these through masturbation, but Israfel was well aware that this was a sin. Moreover, he knew that people generally masturbated to conceived ideas, fantasies that excited their interest, but Israfel's body seemed to follow no logic at all. He would find himself hardening in math class, when young Mr. Sloane stretched up on his toes to write on the chalkboard. Baseball games often had a similar effect on him, even though he loathed organized sports. More worryingly, it sometimes happened during study sessions with Jake or Finn, and frequently when he lay in the darkness with Michael, telling tales of the other realms in his mind.

Something about Israfel's body, then, was "wrong."

Michael, for all his easy popularity, was always a good boy, exceptionally so, and Israfel was entirely sure that he would never touch Alice inappropriately. The fact remained, though, that something in him wanted to, some animalistic, amoral part of his being, which Michael's moral mind controlled. Israfel could see it in the way Michael sometimes looked at her, in the way his fingers curled impotently into the fabric of her T-shirt when he hugged her—just below the swell of her breast, an inch this side of chaste.

He kissed her gently, but Israfel saw the wanting in his mouth, the potential energy behind the warm press of lips against lips. Anyone else, maybe, would only have seen a good Catholic boy, but Israfel *knew* Michael, and he saw right through him.

There were no clues as to why that wanting was absent in Israfel. They were the same, weren't they, after all? The same cellular structure to both of them, the same eyes and nose and fingers, the same beating heart. One Saturday morning, when they'd swum twenty lengths of the local pool, Israfel scrutinized his brother as he toweled himself, looking for answers. Their musculature was a little different, maybe. Israfel swam more than Michael did, and Michael had recently started playing football at school. There wasn't more of it on Michael, though, nothing to suggest a heightened level of testosterone or anything along those lines. He had more of a tan than Israfel, but that was superficial. The muscles in Michael's legs stood out as he shifted, oblivious.

Israfel mapped the breadth of his shoulders, the taper of his body to the waist, and saw nothing unfamiliar. His abdomen was gaining muscle, perhaps, and Israfel's eyes traced the line of it down to the smooth insides of Michael's thighs, the heavy hang of his cock. He stopped there for a long moment, considering. Was it bigger than Israfel's? Was that the difference? Was that even possible, with identical twins? He didn't *think* it was bigger. It was just Michael's cock, uncut like his own, and yet somehow not. Israfel had no doubt that penises were all very much alike, his and Michael's more than anyone's, but it looked different, somehow, seeing it on someone else, even someone who was almost his own mirror image. Looked interesting, the weight of it, the shadows. Israfel wondered what it might be like to touch it. To stroke it, as he had so fastidiously avoided stroking his own. He wondered what it would taste like, the head of it under the flat of Israfel's tongue.

"Raf!"

He looked up guiltily, heat flashing across his cheeks at the realization that his own cock was half-hard, crooking upward from its safe place between his thighs. Michael was waving a hand in front of his face, head tilted to the side. "You zoned out or something, there. You all right?"

"I… yeah." Israfel rubbed a hand across his face, angling his body in what he hoped was a subtle shift to one side. "Sorry. Was just thinking."

"Okay." Michael looked dubious, but he said nothing, and Israfel was grateful. "Pass the towel?"

Israfel passed it and scrambled back into his clothes, still damp. It felt disgusting all the way home, but he was quite sure he deserved it.

After that, it was as if he knew. Oh, he didn't *want* to know, and tried vehemently not to. Tried, even, to tell himself that it was just Michael, just because Michael was his brother and he loved him, and they'd both been part of the same organism to begin with, and their bodies wanted to get back to each other. Then he realized that that was an even worse explanation than the other, and not true besides. Israfel *did* love Michael, and he wanted him to himself in the way that he'd had him when they were kids. Undoubtedly, that had confused him somewhere along the way, the loneliness and thwarted feelings of possession churning themselves into the mix along with his subverted desires. But the point was—and Israfel soon became unable to deny it—that it wasn't because they were Michael's that Israfel sometimes thought those things about his brother's cock, about his mouth and his hipbones. It was because Michael was a boy, and Israfel was hormonal and unable to compartmentalize. What he wanted—what he *really* wanted—was a boy's mouth on his, rough scrape of stubble against his cheek, and then a cock in his mouth, heavy and hard. It just so happened that Michael was the closest available boy and the only one he had ever felt especially strongly about.

The realization, having been made, could not be unmade. The one occasion that he'd tried to talk to Michael about it had been disastrous. They'd been squashed up together on Michael's lower bunk, their hands tucked behind their heads. Israfel had been reading *Amis et Amiloun,* as part of a recent surge of interest in chansons de gestes, and Michael seemed to have responded well to it, laughing and encouraging as Israfel described the fit of the bondsmen into Otherworld. They'd fallen quiet, afterward, Michael still smiling quietly up at the underside of Israfel's bunk above them.

Tentatively, Israfel said, "Why'd you think they'd do all that stuff?" Michael's bare foot was resting against his ankle, and he nudged at it idly. "You know. Sacrifice everything for each other. To be together."

Michael shrugged expansively, curling his toes against the smooth skin on the inside of Israfel's ankle. "Dunno. Because they loved each other, I guess. You know. Soldiers get like that. War builds the strongest bonds, and all that."

"Yeah." Israfel frowned a little, pushing one hand through his hair. "You ever think maybe they, you know, *loved* each other? Like... like, boy-girl loved each other?"

Michael snorted and looked at him sharply. "You mean like faggots?" He drew his foot away, and Israfel felt the chill growing where it had been. "Don't be stupid, Raf. This was medieval France. They were an incredibly religious people. No immoral factions, telling everyone it's okay to go around sinning like that." He huffed through his nose. "Christian men don't feel like that about each other."

"I do." The words were out before Israfel had even properly thought them, and they sounded terribly loud in the quiet of their room. He reached up in horror, pressing his fingers over his mouth. "I mean."

"You what?" Michael wriggled up onto one elbow, staring down at Israfel as if he'd suddenly grown another head. "What are you talking about? You haven't been... *Raf!*"

"No!" Too loud, again, but Israfel was on the edge of panic. He forced himself to breathe, calming himself. "No. I just...." He hesitated. "Sometimes, I... I think about it." He could feel himself flushing, but it was too late to retreat now. "I don't... I'm not interested in girls, Michael. I've tried, but I can't... I mean, I just *don't*. But boys, sometimes...." He trailed off, shaking his head. "I think I'm cursed, Michael." He pressed his hands to his face. "I think I'm... homosexual."

It was the first time he'd ever said it aloud, in any context. In reference to himself, it felt like a firebrand, like an anvil, crushing.

"Oh, Raf." He'd half expected fury, but Michael didn't sound angry so much as pained, like his heart bled for his brother. "Oh, man. *No.*" He reached out to take Israfel by the shoulders and shook. "You're not. Not you. It's... it's sinful; it's horrible; it's something atheists make up to offend decent people. You... you just haven't finished growing yet, okay? Sometimes guys think weird things when they're our age; it doesn't mean anything. It's just like... like a phase, you know?" He clapped his hand down on the flat of Israfel's shoulder, hard. "You're my *brother*. You're not that way. I promise. All right?"

It wasn't all right. Michael was close and concerned and Israfel wanted to cry, and also to pull him close and cling the way they used to, back when they were small. Except he couldn't, now, not with this *thing* between them, his sin and his burden. But Michael had looked so scared for a moment there. There was no other word for it, and Israfel didn't want him to be scared. And after all, maybe he was right. Maybe this was only for now, and one day Israfel would be able to move past it, to make friends with a girl and want to kiss her the way he sometimes wanted to kiss Michael, or Jake, or Finn. Michael was so very sure.

So he said, "All right," with a half smile that promised things he couldn't even begin to feel. "All right."

Michael didn't seem to notice the hollowness. Not then.

For a long while after that, Israfel tried his very hardest to forget about it, to move beyond the phase. He took cold showers when his dick decided to get inappropriately hard—stared at the tile and blanked his mind, scrubbing it clean of whatever had prompted it this time. Michael's hands, perhaps, shafting idly up and down the neck of a Coke bottle, or the way Mr. Sloane's suit trousers stretched across his backside when he moved. Finn, sometimes, smiling at him sidelong, the tone of his voice and the fall of his hair and the warm, spice-sharp smell of him. They were stupid things, misleading things, put in his mind by the devil, and Israfel blanched them all away in cold water.

Increasingly, though, he thought of Finn. Finn and the way his smile dimpled his cheeks when he was properly, truly happy, the clear green of his eyes outside in summer. Israfel loved his eyes, loved green eyes because of him. He thought of Finn's hips, the spurs of bone protruding from his low-slung jeans, and Finn's back, his shoulder blades tapering like wings. Finn was a beautiful thing as Israfel saw him, all soft hair and gently teasing expressions, and Israfel saw him often. In class, in study hall, at somebody's house after school, cramming Spanish on their fronts on the living room floor. Finn made Israfel warm all over, and it wasn't going away.

He hadn't begun to decide what to do about this before Finn kissed him. It was sophomore year of high school, Israfel remembers, the week before the PSAT. He was a week shy of sixteen, Finn a little older, and Israfel was trying to recall the Spanish for "apartment."

Finn laughed at his hesitation. They were lying together on the living room floor on their elbows, shoulders pressed together. Their feet brushed against each other idly, and Israfel had no idea at all what the heck the word was that he'd somehow lost.

"You yield?" Finn asked him, nudging his shoulder hard with his own.

"Yeah," Israfel said, conceding. A thrill leaped in his stomach at Finn's closeness, but he was used to that by now and could ignore it. It was quite useless. "Yeah, I yield, okay? I have no clue. I give in. You win."

"Uh-huh," Finn said, his eyes warm on Israfel. "I win." He bumped against him again, smiling. "You yield."

"I yield," said Israfel.

Finn kissed him then, over the place where their shoulders touched. Israfel froze for a long, painful second, and then Finn parted his lips, and Israfel gave in to it, surrendered, *yielded*. It went on for a while like that, the two of them breathing shortly through their noses, and then Finn leaned further against him, pushing him down onto his side, and they curled up together, their kisses lengthening with the minutes.

That was all it was that night, all it ever was—kissing—but Israfel felt *himself*, like a round peg that had finally found the round keyhole in which it truly belonged. Afterward, he felt no shame, looking up into Finn's smiling face.

"Hey," Finn said, ducking to kiss the tip of Israfel's nose. "You know it's 'apartamento', right?"

"Huh?"

Finn laughed, the laugh that Israfel loved most about him, the laugh that lit his face like the sun. "The Spanish for 'apartment', doofus. It's just 'apartamento'." He ducked his head, nuzzling at Israfel's neck. "You knew that, right? You just wanted to yield to me." And a kiss. And another.

"Yeah," said Israfel, breath hitching on a startled laugh. It wasn't true, consciously, but maybe underneath, it was. "Yeah, Finn, that was obviously it."

"I knew it," Finn said, and in that moment, Israfel really felt that he did. Finn knew everything about him.

They'd been kissing for two weeks the day Michael found them tangled on his bed.

It had been foolish, really, to bring Finn back to their bedroom, and Israfel knew that. But Michael had been out of town on some kind of football tour, not expected back until late, and Israfel was feeling reckless. For two weeks now, he'd laid off the cold water and shame, letting himself indulge, instead, in guilty jerks of his cock in the shower, pretending his hand was Finn's. He knew, of course, that this wasn't something his parents would ever approve, nor something that would ever bring him to rightness with God. But Finn didn't seem to mind—Finn with his clever mouth and warm hands—and Israfel was weak, lost in the delirious pleasure of finding his interest requited.

Finn's parents were Catholics, but in that hereditary, lackluster kind of way that goes straight past "lapsed" and hovers on the verge of collapsed. Finn, consequently, could have recited the catechism backward but knew it more intellectually than spiritually, as some kind of linguistic exercise. Israfel knew he didn't believe in papal infallibility, nor in the universal validity of dogma. Israfel had never met anyone before who openly proclaimed such things and yet still called himself a Christian. It was confusing.

It was nice, though, too—beyond nice—to lie entangled on the lower bunk with this boy and know that, for all the guilt Israfel felt, Finn was, through whatever miracle, convinced of his own, *their* own, innocence. Israfel didn't understand, but everything in him yearned to.

"Do you believe in God?" Israfel asked, mouth ghosting the line of Finn's cheekbone, fingers curled at his waist.

"Course I do." Finn smiled at him, all straight white teeth, and licked a shimmering line along Israfel's upper lip. "And Jesus, and the Holy Spirit, and the Heavenly Host. But I *don't* believe in St. Paul's right to judge people in ways that Jesus never did. Or in people using tribal laws to complain about things when the Old Covenant was explicitly overridden by Christ. It isn't relevant any more. People wouldn't dream of keeping to all the ancient Jewish laws about mildew and shellfish and polyester-cotton-blend, but they're all over 'boys in love is wrong'."

Israfel's laugh punched out of him in startlement, eyes crinkling with it. "Boys in love, huh?"

"Yeah." Finn leaned forward without an instant's hesitation, sealing his mouth over Israfel's. Israfel raised his hands blindly, tangling them in Finn's hair, let himself be pressed down onto his back, Finn's weight welcome and warm against him. Finn kissed him deep, deeper than they'd ventured before, the flat of his tongue stroking rough over Israfel's, their jaws moving wide and strong against each other. Israfel was hard in seconds, his great pain in being sixteen somehow transmuted into a good thing, a natural thing, and he pressed himself up against Finn, wanting more, wanting all of him, *wanting*.

That was when Michael came in.

Much as Israfel loved Finn's confidence, in himself and in his actions, he was grateful that he made no attempt to make a stand against Michael, to defy the look on his face. Israfel couldn't have dealt with it. He was too caught up in the feeling of his chest melting from the inside out, in Michael's stricken expression.

"I should probably go," Finn said softly. The tone of his voice made it, valiantly, a question. Finn was willing to stay if Israfel wanted or needed him to. But Israfel could tell that he would rather leave, and he didn't think he could discuss this with Michael with Finn still in the room. So he nodded, giving Finn a sad little parody of a smile, and Finn left without another word.

The discussion with Michael was short. There wasn't anything to say. Any thoughts Israfel might have had about this being okay and permissible were devastated immediately by the disappointment in Michael's face. Michael had had faith in his brother, in his ability to fight this, and Israfel had let him down. Of course, one couldn't disregard the dogma. Finn had just never been properly taught. He had knowledge of the Church but no real depth of faith. Michael had faith, a lot of it, and if Israfel had destroyed Michael's faith in him, then at least he could honor their mutual faith in God.

Michael said, "You have to let me help you." Israfel can still hear him saying it, the way his voice broke over the words. The desperation in it. "I can't just let this be the end of it, Raf. I'm not going to abandon you to it if there's anything that can be done."

"Michael, I *tried*." His own voice was wet with sudden tears, damp little shreds of words. "I *tried*. But I can't—"

"Sssh, hey. Raf." Michael surged forward, pulled Israfel unhesitatingly into his arms, and held on. "That's only because you had nobody to help you, okay? I should have helped you. I should've... but I didn't know what to *do*."

Israfel heaved out a long breath and clung to his brother. It wasn't often that Michael held him like this anymore, the way they used to curl up together as children in their crib, in the womb. But Israfel knew that it gave Michael as much a sense of security as it did him, that Michael reached out for his brother when the world felt tilted on its axis, because their unity was an anchor for everything. "Not your fault," he mumbled against the side of Michael's neck. "It's me. I'm *wrong*."

"You're sick," Michael said, pulling back a little and kissing him on the forehead. "It's not your fault. Sick people can't be expected to heal themselves." He reached up, rubbing at the tears on Israfel's cheeks. "Raf, I... I think we're gonna have to tell Mom and Dad." He chewed at his lip. "Okay?"

Israfel's stomach swam nauseously at the thought of seeing Michael's disappointment reflected on both their faces, but Michael was right, he knew. He couldn't fix himself, and he so wanted to be fixed. For Michael, as much as for himself. He nodded, almost imperceptibly at first, and then more definitely. "Yeah, I know. It's okay."

Mr. and Mrs. Vacek, as Michael had anticipated, did have solutions to offer. The Catholic church didn't run camps—they weren't Mormons, or Nazis, Mr. Vacek said with a pained little smile when Israfel suggested it—but there turned out to be a therapy program run by a church in the neighboring diocese that Mrs. Vacek felt might help.

The program was run by the church's Office of Marriage and Family Life and operated on the reassuring premise that "Same Sex Attraction Disorder" was both treatable and preventable. The basic condition of sexual orientation toward those of the same sex was not, Israfel learned, in itself a sin, and people who experienced it were in no way excluded from God's love. Deliberate homosexual activity, however, was an abuse of the sexual faculty and, when engaged in freely and knowingly, was sinful. The ultimate goal of the program was to alter the orientation of the afflicted, but there was a recognition—as there would not have been in other churches—that sometimes the orientation was simply so ingrained as to be inalterable. Israfel, after several weeks of absolute non-response to attempts to interest him, romantically or sexually, in women, was placed in this category. At this point, the program taught, the afflicted person had to recognize that their condition was from God—not necessarily a damning thing, but, rather, a clear call to chastity.

This was how Israfel came to enter the priesthood. The therapy program could not cure him of his homosexuality, but it did teach him how to manage it and insisted, moreover, that he ought to see his enforced celibacy as a gift. In consideration of *why* God might have gifted him with so confusing a condition, then, Israfel came to the conclusion that he was being called to the Ministry. He was, and had always been, a devout boy, whose interest in dead languages and theological history was as great as his genuine engagement with the catechism. His temperament, his mother said when he broached the topic with her, was certainly suited to priesthood. He was quiet, unassuming, kind. People warmed to him. He spoke articulately. And now, of course, he was to be celibate anyway. The priesthood seemed suddenly uplifted like a sign from the heavens of What God Wanted From Israfel.

When he was eighteen, Israfel entered the Seminary of Notre Dame, convinced that he was doing right. Michael wished him goodbye at the door, told him, "I'm proud of you, Raf. I'm so proud of you."

Israfel carried his blessing with him like a talisman, like a charm around his neck.

Nine

THE All Souls' Day Mass is traditionally celebrated with aplomb in this town, a fact of which Israfel's predecessor was certain to make him especially aware. Many churches pay rather less attention to the festival, but here the parishioners expect a midnight Mass, for which the whole congregation shows up in force and without fail.

Israfel hasn't seen much of Nate since The Kiss, or at least not to speak to. He has seen him seated with his parents in their regular pew, but Nate has made no move to hold his eyes or to catch his attention at all. Israfel isn't sure whether this is an attempt on Nate's part to respect his wishes or simply emblematic of the fact that Nate is furious at him for his rejection on the heels of their ill-advised encounter.

The churning in Israfel's gut is constant, a roiling hollowness in his abdomen. It is wrong, he knows, but part of him almost hopes for the fury, as opposed to the acquiescence, the new respect for his celibacy. It is wrong, he knows, but it's been many years since Israfel has personally *mattered* to anyone, even in this most impossible of ways.

Israfel wants Nate, cannot have him but can no longer deny the desire. It had always been easier before, when his crushes went unencouraged, but he can't make himself want that with Nate, doesn't want to be alone with this boiling in his blood.

He supposes this makes him a bad priest and a bad man, but his body/heart/soul don't seem to care.

The church is busy all evening on All Souls' Day: sacristans and bell ringers setting up and practicing their duties, the choir singing scales in the back pews of the church. The altar servers—all four of them, today, with the expectation that Book's arms will wear out halfway through the longer service, and that more candles will mean more help needed—arrive at around eleven. Israfel wonders, idly, whether they've all shown up at once like that because Nate has driven them all here in his car. Certainly, there are no parents yet anywhere to be seen.

"You're going to be Book today, Nate, is that right?" he asks, in challenge to himself. Whichever way things go, they cannot remain like this, with this uncertainty thundering its sickening pulse in his stomach. If Nate is distant, it'll twist in his flesh like a knife, but at least Israfel will *know*.

But Nate just says, "Oh, man, I shouldn't make promises," and grins at Israfel lightly. Israfel feels his face breaking out in an answering smile, almost against his will, and notices Nate noticing. His face is unreadable, green eyes intrigued-amused-wary, and the stone in Israfel's stomach shifts, shivers into something else.

He's going to end up screwed by Nate Mulligan, he thinks, one way or the other. His body is entirely less unhappy with this conclusion than it rightfully should be, heat overriding his mind's enfeebled constraints.

"Book," he tells Nate firmly, in as level a voice as he can manage, and turns away to the sacristy to hide his rising blush.

It's a good service, for all its length, although Israfel's voice has begun to wear thin by the end of it after booming out for so long to the very back of the packed nave. The servers, used as they are to working in pairs, have evidently done their fair share of big services, too, and Nate hands over the missal to Tom with perfect grace at the correct point, takes up the candles when needed, and goes to the aid of the girls when their energy is sapped. Israfel feels a sense of near-parental pride that would have been appropriate had it not been so shockingly out of keeping with all the other ways in which he thinks about Nate these days.

By the time the congregation begins to file out, it's nearly two in the morning, but Israfel has gone past the point of tiredness and into a whole new cycle of energy. Undoubtedly, he will pay the price for it later, but for the time being, he's thrumming with it, a little jittery-drunk, but wide awake. Nate and Tom, who appear to be playing an impromptu game with the candles as they collect them, seem to be in much the same state, eyes overbright despite the shadows beneath them. Anne is carrying the missal away at a rather more sedate pace, and Jessica is leaning, half asleep, against the pulpit. Israfel smiles and goes to her aid.

"Come on, sweetheart. That can't be very comfortable, can it?" He takes her by the shoulders very gently, attempting to shake her back to some form of consciousness, but she only blinks at him blearily and collapses back against the pulpit like a ragdoll. Israfel sighs. He's not supposed to touch children. Everybody knows that. It's a concern these days. But there's nobody around except the other servers, and no sign of Jess's parents, so he lifts her bodily and deposits her in the front pew, where she settles immediately into a doze.

"Don't worry."

Israfel startles at the sound of Nate's voice, so close to his ear that he feels the reverberation under his skin. Nate smiles at him and inclines his head in Jessica's direction. "I'm driving them all home when we're done. Altar servers usually stay behind a while to clear up." He shrugs. "Guess Jess's still a little too young to handle it, huh?"

"How old is she?" Israfel asks, suddenly curious.

Nate contemplates. "Twelve, maybe? Yeah, I think she's younger'n Tommy. And Tommy's got way more stamina than most kids his age anyway."

Israfel's mouth quirks. Sure enough, on the far side of the church, Tom is busily stacking up the collected candles. He reminds Israfel of nothing so much as the fairytale Happy Worker of the old Soviet posters, his face intent and half-smiling. "And why's that?" he asks Nate, smiling.

Nate rolls his eyes and pushes his hands backward through his hair from the forehead. The gesture makes the tendon in his neck stand out, displays the fine bones of his wrists protruding from beneath the sleeves of the surplice. "Much as I hate to admit it, probably Dad. He's big on, you know, 'training'." He snorts. "He's been making us run in the mornings since we were eight. Damn ex-military types. It's his greatest ambition for me to join the freakin' US Army."

"You don't want to?" Israfel asks carefully.

Nate gives him a pointed look. "There's kind of a pressing reason why they wouldn't want me, Padre," Nate says wryly. "I'm sure you can guess it."

Israfel opens his mouth. His mind is suddenly milling with things he wants to say, but he has no idea where to start. In the end, he says, "But you're not... I mean, Tom says you *are* interested in girls."

Nate shrugs. "Sure. But the Army doesn't care how much you like girls if you also like cock."

Israfel feels himself flushing immediately, heat washing up his neck, moving up to his face. "Nate," he says, his voice full of warning. "You know this isn't good for you. It's wrong. And I know you can't...." He takes a breath. "I know you can't ever really suppress that, but at least it's not the only part of you. You'll have to choose one person to marry eventually, and you can choose a nice girl. You can be normal. You have that privilege."

Nate looks at Israfel for a moment, eyes intent and steady. Then he glances across the church to where Tom is now talking to Anne, the two of them systematically packing up the altar. When he looks back to Israfel, his face is set, emphatic. "What if I don't *want* to choose a nice girl, huh? What if that's not my preference?"

Israfel sighs. "Nate, it's that or this." He gestures to himself, hands encompassing the cassock and the rosary, the symbols of his celibacy.

Nate frowns. "Or, you know, it's doing what the fuck you like."

"And being damned for it," Israfel points out firmly.

Nate's mouth twitches, and Israfel braces himself for a sharp retort, another outburst like last time to set them up for another two weeks of uncertainty and awkwardness. But Nate seems to recover himself after a minute. He shakes his head and looks at the floor. "I need some air," he says, voice low and unreadable. "I'll be outside if you need me for anything."

He turns and begins walking toward the sacristy, rucking up his surplice as he goes, shoving his hands into the pocket of his jeans underneath the bunched white fabric.

Every instinct Israfel possesses wants to follow Nate. The rational part of him, the part now wrestling lunacy on a daily basis, cautions strongly against this, and Israfel wraps his fingers around the rosary at his throat, closes his eyes, and says ten Our Fathers until the urge passes and Nate is gone. From his place by the altar, Tom looks up at him, smiling when their eyes meet. Israfel smiles back shakily, raising his free hand in salute.

"Almost done," Tom calls, indicating the neat stacks on the altar. "Where'd Nate go? He's driving."

It's an excuse that Israfel shouldn't leap upon, and everything strong in him knows it. He should send Tom outside to find his brother. He should take over helping Anne, should lock all the doors and turn off the lights for the night. But the core of him jumps at the chance to follow Nate, to obey his initial inclinations. Israfel would resist, but it's late, and all his nerves are wound too tight, and wisdom isn't easy when it's almost 2:00 a.m.

"I'll fetch him," Israfel hears himself saying. "Just finish up here, will you, you two?"

The sacristy is a small room whose unusual shape suggests that it possibly used to fulfill some other purpose. At the back of the room is a door leading onto an enclosed area behind the church where the garbage cans live, a partially walled-off little yard. When Israfel enters the sacristy, he notices immediately that this door is open, the cool November air filtering sharp and clean into the building.

"Nate?" he calls cautiously. He waits a moment, but there is no response. The open door is a rectangle of total darkness, the yard unlit and silent beyond it. Israfel sighs and crosses the room toward it.

He can feel Nate long before he sees him, his living essence tangible in the chill of the yard. Israfel stands on the doorstep, squinting out into the darkness, and waits for his eyes to adjust.

"You need me for something?" Nate asks.

Israfel follows the sound of his voice. The darkness is less complete, now, to his eyes, and Nate is visible as a pale shape in it, his back against the wall of the church. There's a little orange speck glowing somewhere near his face, and when Israfel takes a step toward him, he catches the smell of used-up smoke and rich loose tobacco.

"We don't smoke in the church," Israfel says.

The glowing speck moves a little. "That's cool," Nate retorts. "We're not smoking in the church. *I* am smoking outside of it." He pauses, huffs out a laugh, and then holds out the cigarette, the pulsing orange end of it suddenly rather closer to Israfel's face. "Although you're welcome to join me."

"I don't smoke," Israfel says politely. It's an automatic response, and he's grateful for it because the thought is suddenly very appealing: the end of the cigarette damp from Nate's lips; Israfel's fingers around the place where Nate's have been.

Nate shrugs, the shape of the motion detectable in the dark. In the surplice, he looks otherworldly, the white cloth shimmering. "Neither do I," he says and puts the cigarette back in his mouth. "I just have an oral fixation," he explains around it.

Something hotly inappropriate is attempting to climb out of Israfel through his throat, and he swallows hard against it. "Nate," he says, softly. "What I... what I said...."

"What you said," Nate echoes softly, pointlessly. He drops the cigarette, grinds it out under his shoe. Then his hands are on Israfel's shoulders, turning him gently. Israfel's mind is blurred by tiredness and adrenaline, and he lets himself be moved. The next thing he knows is the roughness of brick at his back and Nate's mouth brushing, barely felt, against his jaw. He draws in a sharp breath.

"What you said is bullshit, Father," Nate says, and curls his tongue into the space behind the bolt of Israfel's jaw, sending a shiver coiling down his back. "I shouldn't have yelled at you last time; I know that. But...." His fingers trace the line of Israfel's collar, the soft skin of his neck above it. "You're wrong. Your God wants you to have nice things, right?"

Nate is close to him, so close, the length of his body warm against Israfel's, and Israfel bites down hard on his lip with the effort of holding still, not touching. "I *have* nice things," he hisses desperately. This is his last chance, his last attempt, and he knows it, voice breaking with the realization. Nate is chiseling systematically through Israfel's slow-built walls, and Israfel hasn't the strength to throw up any more. He's never been pursued like this, never been so *wanted*, and this intensity of feeling coming from outside of himself leaves his old defenses powerless against it.

"Nate," he says, "This is not a 'nice thing'. This is Satan, tempting us as he tempted Christ in the wilderness. We have to overcome it." He grips Nate's shoulders, shakes them. "It's a *chance*. To prove ourselves."

He used to believe it at one point. He honestly, genuinely did. But even as the words leave his lips, Israfel's faith in them is wavering. He can feel Nate's skepticism like a stone wall in the dark. On the one hand, in front of him, there is Nate, all heat and conviction; and on the other, the memory of Michael, the disappointment in his face.

Israfel hasn't seen Michael in almost two years. Nate and his immediacy are winning out.

The curve of Nate's smile against Israfel's face says he knows it. Israfel doesn't know what gives him away—the tone of his voice, maybe, or the racing of his heart, so loud he feels that Nate can't help hearing. Maybe he doesn't know, and it's only because he's Nate, resolute and certain as Israfel has never been. But Nate's response is a growled "I'll show you a 'nice thing'," harsh and heated against Israfel's ear. Then there's a brief, firm press of his mouth to Israfel's, and the next thing Israfel knows, Nate's on his knees on the damp concrete.

"Nate," Israfel says, but it's too late and far, far too little. Nate's sliding his palms firmly up Israfel's legs, forearms lifting the vestments with them as they rise. His hands are warm, too warm, through the fabric of Israfel's trousers, and Israfel's body is frozen in place, breath hitching shallowly as Nate's thumbs skirt his inner thighs.

Nate doesn't linger. He knows, perhaps, that delaying will do nothing but give Israfel's nerves a chance to rally and run. Furthermore, there are children in the church, awaiting them, and the November air is sharp, the small hours unfolding around them. At any rate, Israfel has barely finished drawing breath when he feels Nate's thumb rub over his zipper, smoothing it painful but good against the hardness beneath.

The sound that escapes him is involuntary, as is the reflexive clenching of his fingers in Nate's hair, but Nate seems not to mind. There's a catch in his breath, too, which might be a laugh or might be something else, and then he's nuzzling at Israfel with nose and cheekbone, rubbing his face, catlike, against him.

Israfel does move, then, a whimper strangled out of him as his hands tug, frantic, at Nate's hair, jolted into terror by the reality of Nate's warm cheek pressed against him. But Nate is ready for him, and he moves quickly, thumbing down the zipper and jerking forward out of Israfel's grip, mouthing at him damply through the thin cotton of his undershorts.

A flash of heat, and Israfel has lost his mind.

Nate takes advantage. Israfel is, to his own shame, straining right to the waistband of his shorts, and Nate wastes no time in dragging the fabric down over his swollen cock. The night air is a shock of cold, setting his pulse thundering, but he has only a moment to feel it. Nate's tongue—his *tongue*, and the thought makes Israfel want so hard he can barely breathe—traces a brief, ticklesome path from root to tip, where he paints circles in Israfel's wetness. Israfel's hips jerk wildly, and Nate laughs, pins them flat to the wall by the hipbones.

"Easy, Father," he says softly, "I got you. Just be patient a second."

Israfel hardly has time to register self-loathing before Nate's mouth envelops him entirely, sliding down him in a rush of wet heat, and his brain loses hold of everything else. Nate is *good* at this: opening his throat to the shallow, stuttering thrusts of Israfel's pinned hips; sucking hard until Israfel feels himself abruptly on the edge of an abyss: and then withdrawing, letting his mouth go loose as his tongue traces patterns on the underside of Israfel's cock. Israfel can't tell why it feels so good—whether because Nate has had a lot of practice, or only because nothing has ever touched Israfel's cock but his own hand, and even that infrequently—but there are no nicks of teeth, no hesitations. This is very, very clearly not Nate's first time at this. Israfel has the distinct impression that Nate knows a number of different ways to… to stimulate a man orally, and that this one is the Fast, Mind-blowing Explosion.

Nate doesn't tease. There are edges of teasing to his actions, to make it, as Nate said, "nice," rather than simply a short, violent culmination before Israfel has had the opportunity to experience the skill of Nate's mouth. But for the most part, he works steadily, intensely. Takes Israfel deep and sucks hard for a moment at the base before he pulls off, still sucking, corkscrewing a little as he nears the tip. Then, a firm press of Nate's tongue to the sensitive crown of him, working right into the slit, and it begins again. Slide down, suck, pull up, tongue, and Israfel is dissolving under it. His mind is dissolving, his *bones* are dissolving. The silence of the yard is broken by his choked-off whimpers, and there is nothing he can do about it. Nate's too good at this, too incredibly fucking good, and Israfel feels as if every flicker of sensation in his body has been diverted into his cock, Nate's tongue somehow touching every lost part of him as he works.

He has both hands in Nate's hair, pulling too hard, and it's rude, he knows it is, but Nate is already as close as he can get, and Israfel doesn't seem to be breaking his stride with his tugs. Israfel is *there*, right there on the edge of everything, pelvis rocking incrementally and instinctively as his head falls back against the damp brick of the wall, the crest of the wave building white and shining inside him, everywhere. And then Nate releases his hips, and Israfel's next thrust carries him deep to the back of Nate's throat, and the wave breaks, just like that, floods him with light and looseness and triumph, even as he floods Nate's mouth with pulse after pulse of ejaculate. He cries out, not loudly, but something, because he can't not, and then Nate is licking at him, swallowing around him, and pulses of pleasure speed through him in hot little aftershocks. Israfel collapses back against the wall and gasps for breath.

"Nice, huh?" Nate's voice is rough and warm, pride and arousal competing in it. Israfel blinks dazedly, unable to speak; unable, even, to feel anything just yet but the pounding of his heart. Nate tucks him back into his shorts, refastens his trousers, rearranges his cassock. When he stands, he leans in immediately to press his mouth to Israfel's, and it ought to be repugnant, the bitter salt taste of himself laid over Nate's tongue, but Israfel, clearly, is lost to madness because it isn't. It doesn't excite him, exactly— especially not now, with his limbs all like jelly—but it's warming somehow, intimate. Israfel exhales shakily through his nose and sucks on Nate's tongue.

Nate pulls away after a long moment, half laughing. "Just a second, Padre." He's fumbling with something, and it takes Israfel a second to realize that he's pulling out his own cock, cradling it. "Can't go back in there like this." He grips tight, torques his wrist as he tugs upward, and then slides his hand down again.

Israfel doesn't know what makes him do it. It's involuntary, unintended, but he's never been with another man this way, and the smell of sex is everywhere. He wants, he *wants* to push Nate's hand away; wants, through some unhinged sex insanity, to go to his knees until the taste of Nate explodes in his mouth too. But Nate is stroking himself, steady and breathless, cock slipping through his fist with fast slick sounds, and Israfel can only do what he dares.

At the first touch of Israfel's fingertip to the crown of him, Nate comes. It bursts out of him sudden and hot, coating Israfel's hand, Nate's hand, the ground; and a sound is torn out of Nate with it, guttural surprise and affirmation. Nate is so warm, and Israfel feels his body flushing again, skin prickling in sympathetic, almost phantom, arousal. Nate is beautiful, so beautiful, and Israfel can make him come with just a fingertip touch. The rush of self-satisfaction is so great that, for a moment, he feels as powerful as God.

Then Nate's mouth is on his hand, sucking at Israfel's fingers one by one, and Israfel shudders.

"Fuck," Nate rasps out, "You didn't... *fuck*."

He wipes his own hand on the back pocket of his jeans and then refastens his fly. Israfel folds his own hands, the fingers of the right one still spit damp. They stare at each other, eyes glinting palely in the dark.

Neither of them speaks. Israfel feels sure that he has somehow upset Nate's great plan with his (apparently unanticipated) participation, that Nate is thinking too hard, now, to have anything to say. He can hear him thinking, looking for some smart-aleck remark, but there is nothing. Israfel has nothing either.

Tom's voice from the door makes them both jump. "Nate? You out here?"

Nate curses softly under his breath and pulls away from Israfel. "Yeah! Yeah, Tommy, I'm out here. Sorry."

He tosses a glance at Israfel, unreadable, and then steps into the sacristy. Israfel gives him a moment, then follows. He is tired now—suddenly and intensely exhausted—and it's worse in the warmth inside of the building.

"We'll be off," Nate says, jabbing his thumb in the direction of the nave. To Tom he says, "Where're the girls?"

"I opened the car for them," Tom tells him. "You left the keys in your jacket pocket." He snorts. "I would have just gone home without you, but—"

"Feet don't reach the pedals yet. I know, squirt." Nate gives his brother a little shove and then hauls him close again with an arm around his neck. Tom looks tired now, too, dark circles under his eyes and a slump to his shoulders. He says nothing in response to his brother, just leans heavily against him and lets himself be supported.

Israfel crosses his arms awkwardly. "Well," he says. His own voice sounds strange to his ears, somehow roughened. "Don't forget your jacket then."

"Won't," Nate says. There's a beat of nothing, as if he's thinking about it, but then he smiles at Israfel, and Israfel feels himself smiling back. "You all right finishing up here?"

Israfel shrugs. "It's mostly done, thanks to you and Anne, Tom. I'll finish in the morning." He laughs shortly. "*Later* in the morning, I suppose."

Nate nods. "Sounds good." He gives Tom a little shake. "C'mon then, Tommy." He takes a step forward, but Tom barely moves. Nate laughs. "C'mon, man, what are you? A horse? Can't sleep standing up."

"M'not," Tom says drowsily. Nate rolls his eyes elaborately at Israfel and scoops Tom up onto his hip as if he were much younger. Tom is still small for his age, but his legs dangle, far too long to curl around Nate's waist the way they must have done once. He seems too out of it to mind, though, looping an arm around Nate's neck and clinging. Nate holds him up with one arm, stooping to pick up his jacket with the other. It doesn't look as if it's causing him any great difficulty, and that knowledge—of how strong Nate is—fills Israfel with an entirely inappropriate sense of admiration.

He clears his throat, leans against the doorframe as Nate steps out through it. "I, uh. Thank you for coming."

His cheeks flush even as he says it, but it's too late. Nate smiles back at him, though, the crook of it pleased, and also, Israfel thinks, maybe just a little embarrassed.

He doesn't know why that makes his stomach curl with pleasure, but it does.

"It was my pleasure," Nate says. "See you later, Padre."

"It's Raf," Israfel calls after him as he turns away. He doesn't know what makes him say it—he hadn't meant to—but it just comes out, and the grin on Nate's face when he turns around again is so blinding as to absolutely justify it.

"Well," Nate says. "Night, Raf. Sweet dreams."

The sound of it on Nate's lips—that nickname that feels, to Israfel, like his real self, the part of him that was obliterated at his ordination—makes him shiver. He clutches it to himself as Nate walks away, as he watches the car drive off into the darkness. It flutters in his blood like wine, making him lightheaded, and he laughs a little drunkenly into the emptiness.

"This is the way the world ends," Israfel thinks as he retreats into the church, and the words do not ring hollow in him as they should. *"This is the way the world ends/ Not with a bang but a whimper."*

Ten

ISRAFEL sleeps until three in the afternoon. Early Monday masses are usually canceled after a midnight event, and Israfel is grateful for it. When, at length, he comes back to a bleary form of consciousness, he's still a little groggy, out of it from the night before.

The late Mass… and other things.

He doesn't think about it, beyond superficially. As he pours himself black coffee, leaning against the countertop in a T-shirt and soft pajama bottoms, he thinks of Nate's hair slipping between his fingers but stops himself short of the "whys" and "therefores." As he sits, feet tucked under him, mug cradled between his palms, he remembers the heat of Nate's mouth but does not let his mind go beyond the flesh.

When his doorbell chimes at a little after five, Israfel is still in his mussed pajamas, entirely unfit to receive visitors. Not even, *especially* not, Nate. But it *is* Nate on the other side of the door, and Israfel knows it even as he crosses the room, long before a glance through the peephole confirms his supposition. It is Nate: green eyes, soft hair, leather jacket, and Israfel seems unable to do anything but the inadvisable when Nate is around these days.

He opens the door. For a long moment, they simply stare at each other while time, like a dribble of wax, slows to a halt and stills, solidifies. Then Israfel abruptly steps back into the room, and Nate steps with him, eyes still burning their unwavering green into his. It is as if the world has narrowed to some strange, echoing thing, all overbright colors and underwater silence. Nate's footsteps on the carpet are soundless, soft. The door snicks softly shut, too, under Israfel's hand. Nate's breathing, though, Israfel hears the labored, shallow pattern of it echoing in his ears. Nate's fingers come up, dreamlike, to twist in the front of Israfel's T-shirt, and then the sound of his breath is too close, too rough. Israfel doesn't even think as he leans forward to swallow the sound, cradling Nate's nape as he opens his mouth over his.

The first touch of their mouths is like breaking surface, the world surging back into motion in a rush of sound and fury. Nate is *there*, suddenly, panting earnestness against Israfel's tongue, and his hands map patterns over Israfel's back through cotton. Israfel hears himself: the pounding of his pulse in his ears, the wet sounds of his lips and tongue, the scritch of his fingernails through the soft hair at the base of Nate's skull. Nate tastes sweet and bitter, as Israfel had dreamed him once—dark with coffee and sweetened by sugar and cream. Israfel pulls him closer, gripping at the back of his head, at his waist, and then Nate is shoving at him, buying space in which to shed his jacket like a skin. It's only a moment of distance, but it's a moment too long before Nate hauls Israfel back against him by his shirt, turns them so Israfel's back smacks soundly against the door. Israfel is reckless, mindless, nipping at Nate's mouth, and he shoves his hands up under Nate's shirt, palming warm skin.

In that instant, a cascade begins. *Cascade*, like a rush of something Israfel cannot stop, does not dare try to. *Cascade*, like the cascade failure of every part of him that was trained so well to say "no." Nate's skin is so smooth, finely milled over his spine and shoulder blades, and Israfel wants to worship him as a miracle, as one of the glories of God. When he starts to pull the shirt up Nate's torso, Nate lets out a strangled sound, a low, incredulous moan. He drags the tee over his own head in less than a second, hooks his hands under Israfel's hem, and Israfel lifts his arms obligingly, needing to be free of his trappings. When he lowers his hands again, they're skin on skin, and it feels like dying.

The stumble across the room to the sofa is by mutual agreement. They collapse with Israfel underneath and Nate straddling his lap, pelvis to pelvis. It's not the most comfortable position—Israfel's neck aches a little as Nate thrusts his tongue into his mouth—but it's worth it for that closeness, the dizzying press of Nate's hardness to Israfel's own, making his head swim with every minute movement.

The movements don't remain minute. The force of their kisses is enough to rock their bodies into each other, and soon enough the seesawing motion turns into grinding, Nate rolling his hips down into Israfel's, Israfel straining upward to maximize the friction in each thrust. Their hands are everywhere—palming shoulders and spines, shallow scrape of nails from nape to waist and back again—and their kiss is like an act of war, aggressive and relentless. Nate is breathing harsh and shallow through his nose, thumbing at Israfel's jaw as he plunders his mouth. Israfel thrusts back at him, not resisting but dueling, challenging, biting Nate's lower lip as he sucks on it. It's madness, violent and rough and thrilling Israfel like electric current in his bloodstream, but he can't stop, and nothing in him wants to.

Then Nate's fingers slip below the waist of his pants, and Israfel remembers that there's more to this, his body latching onto the prospect instantly. Nate's touching him only barely, tips of his fingers stroking the down at the base of Israfel's spine, but the shock of it spirals right into his core, hooking him on a knife-edge of want.

Up, he thinks, curls an arm around Nate's waist and lifts him, shoves him back. Nate's feet flatten on the floor, surprised, and Israfel takes the opportunity to haul himself upright, walking Nate backwards from the sofa with both hands at the small of his back.

Israfel's barely aware of what he's doing, but Nate seems to catch on almost more quickly than Israfel does himself, his look of confusion transmuting into a smirk as he clasps his own hands around the nape of Israfel's neck. He looks almost coquettish, and the thought makes Israfel smile.

"Hmm?" Nate queries, noticing.

Israfel doesn't want to talk. He pulls Nate against him, licks his mouth open and thrusts them back into a kiss.

As it turns out, kissing and walking are difficult feats to achieve simultaneously, even for an excellent multitasker like Israfel. The kissing becomes even sloppier when Israfel begins to fumble open the fastenings of Nate's jeans, such that by the time they back into the bed—there's a guestroom blessedly located on the ground floor, only one room away from the sofa—they aren't kissing so much as breathing wetly against each other's mouths.

For the first time, as Nate's calves meet the firm resistance of the bed, Israfel feels a flicker of hesitation, a jolting flash of his *sensible* mind, crying out in warning from wherever this insanity has trapped it. But Nate is not hesitant, simply uses their momentum to carry him onto his back on the mattress, pulling Israfel with him. And then, Nate is underneath him, and there is no space for sense.

Nate's skin is almost nacreous under Israfel's fingers and mouth, something iridescent in it, glowing like the skin of a pearl. The sounds Nate makes as Israfel touches him are just as beautiful, and Israfel chases them, unthinking. Nate's jeans are most of the way down his thighs, now, and the undulation of his body is focused mostly, Israfel knows, on getting rid of them the rest of the way, but the motion feels amazing against him. He rocks down against Nate's hip, finds the shallow of it and thrusts into it, the soft cotton of his pajama bottoms barely a barrier at all. When the jeans are gone, tangled around Nate's ankles with his boots, there is more of Nate to touch: long swaths of skin down his flanks, up his thighs.

"Raf," Nate whispers. He rubs his mouth open against Israfel's jaw and flicks his tongue over the line of it. "C'mon, Raf." He torques up his hips, dirty and hard. "Here."

He hooks his thumbs under the waistband of Israfel's pants, grazing his hipbones, and Israfel bucks down hard against him in reaction. Nate laughs softly and shoves the garment down and off in one fluid motion, shifts to get rid of his own undershorts before Israfel has caught his breath again, and then...

"Nate," Israfel's grinding out, "Nate, oh God, *Nate!*" and the flat of Nate's pelvis is *so* much more perfect naked.

Nate makes a hot little sound in his throat, fingers raking down Israfel's back to his waist, his backside, holding them together. His knee shifts so that Israfel fits easily between, their cocks moving against each other's stomachs in frictive slides, and Israfel moans.

"Yeah," Nate encourages, "Fuck, yeah, feels good, don't it? So fuckin' wet for me...."

And he is. Dear God, he's smearing his own slickness in the hollow beneath Nate's hipbone, thrusting back and forth in it, but Israfel can't bring himself to care. Nate's wet, too, the hot, slick tip of his hot, hard cock painting lines of fire on Israfel's skin, and that's the way it's *meant* to be. Israfel's vision is blurring, the sensation, still unfamiliar, rising up from his gut, and he grips Nate's hips, half lifts him, pulls their bodies more firmly together.

"Jesus Christ," Nate rasps out jerkily as Israfel speeds his thrusts, increases his force. "Jesus *fucking* Christ don't stop, don't stop, I gotcha, *come on*, fuck, want it, want you all over me—" and it's all Israfel can take.

He flies apart like a mirror dashed on stone, in a thousand shimmering fragments scattering from a point. It's like before, the sensation tearing through him, but *better* because now there is so much of Nate against him, against his chest and thighs and mouth, Nate jerking and gasping as he thrusts again, again, and then arches into climax. There's nothing elegant about it, this schoolboy rutting and smearing of their slickness between their abdomens, but Israfel can't care about that, not with Nate's fingers combing weakly though his hair, Nate's breath panting hot into his mouth as they shudder through the pulses.

Afterward, it's as if Israfel's limbs have melted, passed through fire and become unformed, useless and lax on the bed and around Nate. He waits for it to pass, waits to come back to himself, but for long minutes, he just… doesn't. Nate doesn't move, either, for a time, and Israfel is on the edge of sleep when Nate eventually wriggles out from under him, rolling Israfel firmly onto his side.

Israfel groans. "What you doing?" he mutters ungrammatically, the first word a blurred mess of sound. The sheets are warm against his cheek, and he nuzzles them idly. He feels oddly as if, even with the removal of the frantic animal craving that had driven him before, his body has been stripped down to only its primal urges, its senses and its needs. The sensation of cotton on his skin is good, as is the clean-linen smell, the heat of Nate's hand on Israfel's hip.

Nate laughs shortly. "You wiped?"

"Nnngh," says Israfel.

He knows, knows even through the haze of detachment, that he ought to be thinking more about this. The mounting sense of *wrongwrongWRONG* is screaming to a climax behind the wall that's grown up in his brain to keep all the reasonable parts of him at bay. But although he can feel it there, it's like a new scab right now, something niggling at him with pressure he can almost taste. But the slightest touch is enough to tell him it's too raw, not something he's brave enough to dislodge. It'll sweep over him in dark waves of guilt, and he knows that, he *knows*. He'll have to examine it sometime, but once he does, it will not be shoved away again, and all Israfel wants is this drifting feeling, just for a little while.

Nate, at least, seems happy to let him drift. "It's okay," he says, and Israfel is strangely pleased to note that his voice is drowsy, too. "Happens."

And there it is again, that casual tone in Nate's voice that says he's done this a thousand times before. That this, to him, is nothing particularly special and certainly not something reserved for Israfel. But that, too, threatens pain when he ventures toward it, and Israfel doesn't have the energy.

"We can just lay here for a bit," Nate continues. He shifts, though, fumbles around a little, and it takes Israfel a moment to remember that they'd never quite reached the stage of unlacing Nate's boots, hauling them and his jeans and socks from his person. Nate's doing it now with fingers that have steadied again, efficiently loosening the bootlaces from toe to ankle and then shucking the whole jumble of garments to the floor. He hooks his legs lazily back up onto the bed afterward, wriggling forward until his front is curled against Israfel's back, the pan of his pelvis a perfect cradle for the curve of Israfel's backside. His stomach is a little tacky, their skin adhering where the stickiness is drying, but he's warm and reassuring, holding Israfel as he has never been held, and Israfel doesn't care about a little tackiness.

"Okay?" Nate says, a soft exhalation of breath against the nape of Israfel's neck. Not pushing, not asking, and Israfel is grateful for it even while some edge of his conscious self, leaking under his defenses, questions this lack of interrogation, wonders whether, maybe, it is simply that Nate still doesn't register the importance of this. To Israfel. To *everything*.

Perhaps, says the edge of reason, this is nothing to Nate.

But it doesn't feel like nothing, Nate's warm solidity wrapped around him, and for now, Israfel is willing to be deceived by his senses. *Wants* it, even, for as long as it is still a possibility.

"Yeah," he says, threading his fingers through Nate's. "M'okay."

Nate hums contentedly, rubs his mouth open against the back of Israfel's neck. "Good," he murmurs, and then, "Raf. Fuckin' gorgeous." He moves their joined hands incrementally downward, curling his fingers around the stark jut of Israfel's hipbone.

Israfel feels a flutter of pleasure, blunted by disbelief, but his mind has slipped too far toward sleep to articulate his mixed reaction.

Nate doesn't seem to mind, his body going still against Israfel's but for the rise and fall of his chest. The thrum of his heartbeat pulses against Israfel's back, the warmth of him soothing, gentling, a total and complete embrace.

Israfel is safe with him, for now, and he lets himself fall.

Eleven

WHEN he wakes up, things look very different. In the first place, he wakes to an unexpected darkness, and it feels horribly symbolic. For a moment, he's disoriented, blinking at the pale, fuzzy square of the window in the dimness. Then something shifts behind him, wriggling warm and drowsy against his back, and Israfel remembers. *Nate.*

Realization hits him in a blur that washes over him warmly at first—Nate's hands, Nate's mouth, Nate's skin—and then filters its way through chill to ice, to a frozen stake of fear that spears him through without warning. Nate, and Israfel's broken vow, his broken will. The celibacy of priests is not a doctrine, but a discipline, reliant upon a priest's own continence and self-control—a control inspired and sustained by the priest's exclusive dedication to his vocation. Israfel has never found enough devotion in himself to make his vow what it should be: a sacrifice that is no sacrifice, like a layman's vow of fidelity to a wife he loves. And now his discipline has been exposed for what it is: a feeble thing, built upon shaky ground, weakened by external fixations that have plagued him since childhood.

Israfel was advised, by more than one person, that the priesthood was the best place in which to hide his temperament, but nobody had touched upon the creeping fear that has lurked always at the back of Israfel's mind, the fear that his temperament would not make a life in the priesthood easy. Israfel is a scholar and a classicist, loves Latin and bell ringing and ministering to old ladies. And he loves God; he *does*. But his celibacy, he knows, has always been driven not by sworn dedication to the Church-bride, but by deadly fear of hellfire. If he felt able to marry a woman on fair terms, he has no doubt that he would have done so, with no thought of the priesthood at all. He likes this life, in most ways, but it is a refuge for him, not a vocation.

He has always hoped never to have to consider the implications of this, but now it seems inevitable.

He sighs, shifts a little on the bed. Nate murmurs in his sleep, pressing closer to Israfel's back, and it feels good to have him there, his safe, warm weight.

A man made for the priesthood should not feel lonely, not as Israfel has.

Frowning, he crushes the thought. He is making too much out of this. Israfel is a good priest. He knows it himself, and he has been confirmed in his opinion by parishioners and clergymen alike. Israfel is a good homilist and a good orator, inspirational and intelligent. He can sing the Mass without reference to the missal, and the gospels hold his genuine and unabated interest. The fact that Nate felt so amazing in his arms, the fact that he wanted him, still wants him—this cannot be unique to him, surely? Priests are men, after all. Israfel doubts that many are as asexual as the Church would have them be. Other priests, surely, have these thoughts about women of their acquaintance, imagine their mouths and eyes, their hair and skin, in a mock marriage bed. Some other priests, even, must think this way about other men. They're sinful thoughts, but a man can repent of that. He can say his penance and be forgiven. Clergymen are still human, living in human flesh, and flesh *wants*.

This does not make them unsuited to the life into which they swore themselves as youths.

Most priests, of course, do not touch. Israfel knows this, knows that it would ruin him if this were to come out. Knows that it could ruin him anyway, from within, as it is threatening to do even now. But most priests, he thinks wryly, have not been set upon by Nate Mulligan and his ruthless campaign of youthful beauty and relentless sexuality, playing into every little weakness Israfel has ever had. He should not have given into Nate, but Nate makes him *insane*. Nate is not a bad kid, inherently. Israfel cannot make himself believe that he is, not with the way he smiles, the blatancy of his protective love for his brother. Here, though, he is the unknowing instrument of the Devil, tempting Israfel as Christ Himself was tempted. Israfel has given in once, as Christ never did. But then, Israfel is not Christ, and he is not expected to be.

God is Love. God forgives. He is sick, and his thoughts of Nate are not something he can help. His surrender to them was wrong, but not unforgivable. The Church might say otherwise, but God, Israfel thinks, would not. He is a priest. He is a good priest, and he cannot imagine being anything else.

But this must be the end of it. Israfel has felt the power of temptation, and he must grow beyond it.

When he moves to pull away, Nate moves, too, pressing himself and his half-hard cock to the small of Israfel's back. "Raf?" he murmurs, soft and low and sweet with drowsy confusion.

Israfel's heart clenches. The Plan is so much more *difficult* when Nate is conscious, and Israfel prickles with something horribly close to love for him.

Israfel has always become too quickly attached.

He steels himself and swallows. He wants to press back into Nate's arms, warm around him. He wants to turn and lick into his waiting mouth. But he's done that, given into that, and any further surrender will break him. There is everything, *everything*, Israfel has ever worked for and believed in, and then there is Nate.

Nate is not worth it, not when, to Nate, this is nothing but a youthful challenge, an arrogant desire to attain the unattainable lending a thrill to what must have become humdrum to him. Israfel feels too much, he knows this. He must remember that he's only sex.

Only sex, something cavalier and unimportant to Nate, while it throws Israfel's whole existence into a state of crisis.

The thought makes his throat sour, and in turn, makes his next words come a little easier on the back of the rise of anger. "You need to go," he says quietly and slips off the bed. Nate makes a grab for him, but he's still slow with tiredness, and Israfel is on his feet and fumbling into his pajama pants before Nate is fully awake. "Before anyone misses you."

Nate blinks at him for a moment, slowly. Then he smiles, rolling to his feet, all lazy lines and lithe muscles stretching. "Already?" He raises his arms, as if to curl them around Israfel's neck.

Israfel steps away. It hurts somewhere deep in his gut, but his head is still riding the wave of outrage at Nate's nonchalant attitude, and the heat of it sustains him. "Nate," he says, curtly, "If anyone finds you here, I will be *dismissed*. Do you understand me? I'll be defrocked. I'd never be able to minister again."

He shakes out a T-shirt, abrupt in his irritation, and shrugs it on over his head. It's not the same T-shirt as before, but it was on the floor and handy. "And that's if I'm lucky," he goes on. "If I'm unlucky, I'll be sent to prison too. For corrupting a minor." He snorts. "As if I could corrupt *you*."

He's being harsh, perhaps, but it's the only way. And it's true. Nate is still standing by the bed, expression frozen between two unreadable stages, and Israfel wants to shout at him: *Why did you come here? Why are you* doing *this to me?*

Part of him, though, doesn't want to know the answer.

Nate studies him for a moment and then begins to put on his own clothes. "It was my idea," he says in a low voice.

Israfel sighs. "Yes, Nate, I know."

Nate pauses in the middle of fastening his jeans, apparently at the tone of Israfel's voice, and looks up. There's an expression on his face that Israfel didn't expect to see, something concerned, perhaps, worried, but not in the way Israfel might have anticipated. "You wanted it, though?" he ventures hesitantly. "You didn't... I mean, I didn't...."

It takes a second for Israfel to realize what he's asking. When he does, it's so preposterous that he hardly knows what to say. "No, Nate, you didn't... you didn't *rape* me, for goodness' sake. I consented, though God and all his angels know I shouldn't have. I'm an adult; I *can* consent. You, on the other hand—"

"I'm no virgin," Nate says, quietly. He adjusts his T-shirt, drops to his knees to fasten his boots. He shrugs. "I think I more than consented."

"So do I," Israfel says, more brusquely than intended. "But nobody else will." He indicates the door. "No more of this, Nate, all right. *Please.*"

He holds Nate's eyes for a moment. Nate looks back, and the gold-green gaze is blinding, as always, overwhelming. Israfel sighs and jerks away.

"But you liked it," Nate says gently. He reaches up, touches Israfel's hair, and Israfel, to his shame, cannot pull away. The look on Nate's face is so earnest, so concerned. "Just tell me that. You liked it?"

Israfel sighs heavily and closes his eyes. He cannot look at Nate from this distance and speak reason. It isn't possible. Nate is the most perfect presentation of sin ever created, and Israfel knows he is lost to him, even as he tells himself that this is how it will be. This is how they will skate away from disaster.

"Yes," he admits, because he has to, because he *did*. It was closeness and heat as Israfel has never felt it. It was being with someone in a way he never thought possible. And if it could be like that even with Nate not caring, with Nate just in it for the sheer physicality....

He pushes that thought away too, submerges it and makes himself focus on Nate. "But no more," he says firmly. "All right? I can't. You have to stop."

Nate nods slowly. The rest of his clothes are in the front room, and Israfel follows him as he slips out in search of them, as he shrugs back into his jacket. "I didn't mean to hurt you, Raf," he says. Israfel notices that he does not apologize, but there's sincerity in his voice.

Israfel believes him. He isn't sure what that means.

"Go home," he says. He touches Nate's forehead. "Tomorrow's another day."

"Yeah," Nate says, nodding. He's standing in the doorway, eye to eye with Israfel. His hand is on the door handle. He looks at Israfel for a second and then leans up, slowly, to press a kiss to his mouth. It's gentle, perfect, and Israfel feels his sanity crumbling all over again. "Goodnight, Padre."

Israfel doesn't watch him go. He can't. He goes to the bathroom instead, showers the scent of Nate off his skin, and tries to remind himself why so much the body finds beautiful is evil. Never again, he thinks, turning up his face to the spray. He will never touch Nate again, never feel the rightness of being pulled back against his chest, never run his fingers through his soft hair or kiss his perfect mouth. He will never touch Nate again, and then things will be fine.

Nothing has to change.

Twelve

OF COURSE, it changes everything.

For the first time in a long while, Israfel thinks of his grandmother. When he and Michael were young and Gran would pour them milk cold from the refrigerator or make up batches of pasta for dinner when their parents were out of town, she'd say, "Never had this when I were a lass."

Gran hadn't started life in upstate New York, where Israfel was born. Grandfather Cassidy had married her in England in 1942, when he was a young airman and she was ferrying airplanes for the Women's Auxiliary Air Force. Mrs. Vacek had been born there, before the end of the war, and the little family had not returned to New York until 1946. Gran had still been very young then, and so her voice had picked up a lot of East Coast overlay, but you could still hear the Yorkshire in it. Israfel liked it. It made her different from other people's grandmothers, and all the stories that she told were different too.

He and Michael would query the point about the refrigerator or the pasta, as, of course, she wanted them to do. "Wasn't it weird not having cold drinks, Gran? How could you not have pasta?" And Gran would laugh and say, "You don't miss what you never had, chicks," as if it explained everything.

Now, Israfel begins to think maybe it does. He can't say that he never thought about sexual things before his encounter with Nate, because certainly, on occasion, he did. But they were always wistful thoughts, quickly suppressed, and it was only extremely infrequently that Israfel ever found himself unable to move beyond them without resorting to masturbation. When he did slip in this way, Israfel always confessed his error and did due penance for it. But now... now it's different.

Now when he wakes up hard, he can't seem to disregard it any more, the way he used to, until it went away. Now he lies in his bed and feels the hollow feeling settle in his stomach like a stone, and he twists his fingers in the sheets to keep from touching. Now he lifts his hips, just fractionally, against the coverlet and thinks of the warm tunnel of Nate's mouth, the willingness in his eyes, the way he took Israfel inside himself without a shadow of disgust.

Israfel has long been disgusted with himself. It's strange to know someone who knows the darkness in him and is not repulsed by it. He knows, objectively, that this is because Nate is full of darknesses, too, but he can't *feel* the knowledge. Everything about Nate is golden.

He reminds himself that Nate is an emissary, here to try him. He reminds himself that, if Nate were not so compelling, there would be no temptation to overcome.

The only way to get rid of temptation is to yield to it, recalls Israfel's over-read mind, mocking. *Well, then,* Israfel thinks bitterly. He has yielded. He has succumbed, but he is not rid of it. Nate is with him when he writes his homilies and when he reads his Bible. Nate is with him when he hears Confession, reminding him of his own impurities, transgressions so much greater than Mrs. Carson's white lie to her husband or Peter Sloan's vindictive thoughts about his brother. When he prays the Rosary, sometimes, the shadow of Nate in his mind will become dislodged, and Israfel sinks gratefully into the respite, but he cannot pray forever.

He doesn't last out the week. Nate is as good as his word, makes no contact with Israfel over the course of the next few days, doesn't show up unexpectedly at bell-ringing practice or accompany his mother to her Friday coffee morning. But Sunday is full Mass, and the Mulligans are serving, and there's no way either of them can get out of that.

If Israfel had realized how difficult he would be making things for himself when he insisted that Nate should take Book, he would have let Tom hold the heavy missal until his little arms gave out. Not a very priestly thought, but better than the ones that trip through his head when he's trying to read the service with Nate holding up his words for him, long fingers on the pages in the peripheries of Israfel's vision, his warm, spicy boy-smell somehow more overpowering than the incense. Only because he knows the service even without the missal's prompting does he manage to get through it, eyes averted from the clean lines of Nate beside him, and this is *ridiculous*. His blush stays in place throughout the entire Mass, and Nate's breath is shallow and nervous.

Afterward, Nate corners him in the sacristy. There are candlesticks in both of Israfel's hands, so when Nate steps close, it seems as if there are only two things Israfel can do: hit him with a candlestick or kiss him.

He kisses him. He doesn't mean to, but it seems, in the moment, inevitable. And then, afterward, when Israfel is trying to push Nate away, it works as rather damning currency against him. Nate says, "Raf... please... Raf...." And Israfel turns his face away, says, "God, Nate. You need to go. You need to go."

Nate sucks him off against the bookcase full of school Bibles dating back to the Sunday school that thrived here in the 1960s. Israfel is decked out in full armor, still—pectoral cross and alb over his cassock—but under Nate's scrutiny he feels naked, in every way vulnerable. Nate tries to leave when he's done, when he's kissed

Israfel with salt-sour lips, but it's too late now. If Israfel lets him go like this, his own sense of exposure will only grow. He backs Nate into the wall, swallows his surprised sound, and presses his hand to the tented front of Nate's jeans under the surplice. He thinks Nate tastes of tears, but possibly some of that is the wetness on Israfel's own cheeks, saltwater, like the aftermath of a great pressure, like something being released—horribly, but because it must come out somehow.

Nate kisses him afterward, breathless and grateful and deep, and if Israfel's eyes are still red, he doesn't notice.

Israfel tells himself the same things as before when he gets back to the rectory—makes the same promises, says the same prayers—but the last shred of hope he had of pushing through this, of becoming stronger through his one defeat, is gone. Nate is so warm, and Israfel shouldn't be so cold without him, should be warmed by his Church and his flock, by God, but he isn't. He believes, fervently and desperately, in dogma and catechism, but the dark feeling is growing inside him that he is nothing but a blasphemy of the role he plays, that he is too wrong a man to lead others to do right, as he so wants to do. Israfel has long been a house of cards, and he has been disturbed. He can feel his supports collapsing, day by day.

He can't quite put a finger on when he stops attempting to prop them back up, when the confusion becomes so great that he seems to split in two, one part of him still frantically saying his Rosary while the other rejects the guilt as beyond his capacity to process, simply *does* and *is* and deludes himself. But when he spots Nate's car in his driveway the following evening, he doesn't turn off the lights and go upstairs, as he'd been about to do. He opens the door instead, stands framed in the doorway in his nightclothes, and waits for Nate to get out of the car and come inside. He doesn't kiss Nate until the front door is closed again, but it's a close thing.

There's no madness to it, this time. Israfel cannot claim frenzy as an excuse. Nate's eyes are hot and earnest on his own, but Israfel leads him gently, studiedly, to his bedroom and lets Nate strip them both of their clothes. His skin is prickling everywhere with anticipation, edged with at least a little fear, but Nate's hands are broad and knowing on his cock as they work him, cradling him tight. When they're naked, Israfel somehow ends up straddling Nate's lap, Nate backed up against the pillows. It's the most emasculating position, and Israfel knows it in the yawning well of shame inside himself, but he likes the way Nate's body feels, supporting him like this, likes the way his strength is made evident in the way he steadies Israfel's hips. They kiss like that for a long time, fingers combing through each other's hair, licking deep as darkness into each other's mouths while they roll and shiver against each other. At length, Nate encircles them both in his big, gentle hand, stroking until both of them are boneless and sated and slick.

After that, Israfel gives up thinking. He says his masses and homilies and prayers as earnestly as before, but in the evenings, on weekend afternoons, there's Nate in his bed nevertheless, Nate's mouth and his acres of skin. It's not right, but there's nothing he can do about it, and nobody has to know.

Israfel recognizes his hypocrisy for the cowardice that it is, but his options are few, and none of them attractive. He is damned, he knows. All that remains to be seen is how long he can evade retribution.

When he is alone—when Nate has gone home to tell some lie or other to his parents, when there's only the sound of the clock in the dark to distract him—Israfel thinks it can't go on long. In these moments, it seems that all they are, are twists of immorality and lies, a powder keg poised to explode and take Israfel with it. But sometimes, when they are together, there are parts of him that feel differently. There are days when Nate arrives in the early evening, and for a long time they do nothing but curl around each other on the couch, watching cartoons dispassionately while Nate defends his eclectic taste in literature. And then, too, there are the Sunday mornings in the sacristy with Tom, the three of them lightheartedly teasing each other, when Israfel feels, for the first time in a long time, *part* of something. In these instances, Israfel doubts his own damning judgments—when the connection between them extends beyond the tangle of their limbs into something vibrant and multifaceted, something that feels so real Israfel has trouble doubting it.

For the most part, though, what they have is sex. In Israfel's bed, on his couch, on his floor; after Sunday Mass, after Nate's finished with his lessons, after they've slept off a first round and woken up ready for a second. It's inelegant and irredeemable, sticky and wrong and amazing, and if Israfel feels a little too much at the sight of Nate's face wide-eyed and slack with pleasure… well. That is Israfel's folly. He's always tended to read too much into details.

It can't last long; this, Israfel knows. But Nate is *there*, willing and eager and perfect, and Israfel isn't strong enough anymore to resist him. Mostly, he is skirting the edge of hedonism on the surface of himself, gone loose, while underneath, he anticipates the end.

Thirteen

IN THE event, the end looks like Michael.

It's ironic, really; might almost be funny, if Israfel's concerns weren't so horribly serious. He's in the little downstairs shower, sluicing Nate's emissions off his stomach, when he hears the rumble of voices in the living room outside. He pulls his T-shirt and sweatpants on too quickly, in his curiosity, and stumbles out of the bathroom with them sticking damply to his body, his hair a mess of damp spikes.

"Nate?" he ventures, his voice low and bemused.

"Raf?" comes his own voice, confused and suspicious. Raf lifts his head to see his own face staring back at him, like some judgmental manifestation of his conscience.

He hasn't seen Michael in long enough that it takes him a moment to realize what it is he's seeing. The sudden seize in his chest doesn't loosen any when he works it out.

"Michael?" Israfel says incredulously. "What are you doing here?"

"You never said you had a *twin*," Nate says. He's lounging against the bookcase with his hands in his jeans pockets, fully dressed—thanks be to God—but with a smirk playing about his mouth that promises bad things. Israfel frowns, makes a brief attempt to silence Nate by the power of his eyebrows alone.

"It never came up," he mutters. "Nate, could you...?"

Nate swings himself upright, but neither the hands nor the smirk move a fraction. "Sure thing, Father. We can talk about that parable later, huh?"

Israfel isn't sure which of them is more surprised when Michael puts out a cautious hand, stilling Nate with fingers on the cusp of his shoulder. "You needn't go on my account," he says, his voice still edged with something altogether too close to suspicion. "Just let me talk to my brother a minute, would you?"

"Sure," Nate says, drawing the vowel out dubiously as he glances from Israfel to Michael and back again. "I'll just... go back to that book I left in your study, Padre." He holds Israfel's eyes for a moment and then slips out of the room.

Israfel barely has time to register relief before Michael is advancing, wearing a smile of his own that Israfel doesn't like. It's an expression he knows all too well. Not one that he'd ever wear himself. Strange, how two identical faces can display emotion so differently.

Israfel crosses his arms, the gesture unashamedly defensive. "Michael?"

Michael shrugs. It's elaborate, deliberately casual. "Haven't seen you in a while, that's all. Charlotte and I were wondering about your new parish, and"—he spreads his hands—"it certainly looks nice."

Israfel draws his brows together, tries not to fidget too obviously. "Are they with you?"

It's been some time, after all. Israfel has always been rather fond of Michael's wife—who is cleverer and more interesting, less emptily attractive, than the sort of woman Israfel used to envisage his brother marrying—and still more so of their daughter, Claire. She must be eight by now, he realizes with a start. Two years, at her stage of life, make an enormous difference.

"In the car," Michael says, his voice softening. "Look, I-I'm sorry I didn't call ahead. I should have done, I know that. I just...." He draws his lower lip between his teeth, chewing on it a little, and the gesture is so absolutely Michael that Israfel feels the tension inside him beginning to dissipate. "I just didn't expect you to have company." Michael laughs shortly. "You've never been the 'company' sort, I guess."

Israfel laughs softly, rubbing the heel of his hand across his face. "No, I-I know."

Nate is silent, upstairs, but the memory of his presence there sits like a rock in Israfel's gut, and he shifts uncomfortably. "Nate's just... I mean, I can ask him to come back another time, it's no problem. You just bring the girls in. I'll make you dinner or something?"

He glances at his watch. It's a little after six, which, surely, is dinner time?

"Keen, is he?" Michael nods his head in the direction of the stairs, and Israfel colors, thinking of Nate's eager mouth on him, the needy undulations of his body.

"Very," he says truthfully, and Michael laughs.

"Well, don't throw him out on our account, huh? It might be nice to meet your little protégé. I bet Claire would like him."

Israfel splutters. It's most undignified, but he can't help himself. "Huh? Michael, Claire's *eight*. Unless I've miscalculated somewhere."

Michael smiles. "No, you're right on the money, but she's one precocious eight-year-old. Handsome teenaged boys seem to be right up her street at the minute." He snorts. "I blame television."

Israfel stomps firmly down on the little twist of distaste that rises in his chest. He doesn't want to investigate too closely whether its source is the thought of Claire having an interest in boys so young, or the thought of her having an interest in Nate. As if it matters.

"Well," he says carefully, "I'm not sure if Nate will be able to stay. I wasn't planning on keeping him for dinner." And, really, prolonged exposure of Nate to Michael is the last thing Israfel wants. Michael knows him, better than anyone else in the world, and Israfel doesn't trust himself not to give something away. He trusts Nate with the secret even less.

Michael, though, doesn't seem to take the hint. "Nonsense," he says firmly. "It'd be nice to get to know him, ask him what the parish was like before you came along, all that kind of thing. For, you know, comparative purposes?" He grins and claps Israfel on the shoulder. "Go on, go upstairs and ask him to stay. I'll give you ten minutes to do that and get changed before I bring the girls in."

The look on his face as he walks out leaves no doubt in Israfel's mind that, for Michael at least, this matter is settled. He lets out a heavy sigh into the empty room and turns toward the stairs.

He finds Nate, as promised, in his study, perched on the corner of the desk. Israfel smiles at him wryly as he closes the door behind him. "So," he says, on a long exhale.

Nate looks, for a moment, expectant, and then, when the moment draws on, a little impatient. "*So?* Is he staying?" Nate's face goes from zero to salacious in less than half a second, smirk tugging at the corners of his mouth. "Bet we could do some interesting things with two of you."

"Nate!" The leap in Israfel's heart rate feels like a literal spike, rived up through his throat, and at least ninety percent of it is anxiety. (The other ten percent is irrelevant.) "I don't want to hear any of that, all right? He's my *brother*." He hesitates. "Which, apart from the fact that *he's my brother*, also means that he's had the exact same upbringing that I had. He's very devout. He'd report me in a second if he knew." Israfel sighs heavily, trepidation squeezing his gut with dark fingers. "*I* would report myself in a second, if I was myself. If I wasn't...."

He breaks off, one hand across his eyes. Nate's whole attitude shifts in an instant. He flows off the desk like water, hand coming up to settle on Israfel's shoulder, sliding up to grip the back of his neck reassuringly. "Hey," he coaxes, his voice low and soft. "Hey. It's okay." He scritches a thumb through the soft hair curling at Israfel's nape, and Israfel, despite himself, feels it begin to unwind him.

"It's not okay," Israfel returns gruffly, but he lets Nate's hand stay. He feels suddenly, overwhelmingly exhausted, in that headachey, full-body way that comes after a long and strenuous swim. Michael stirs up his troubles and anxieties, has always done so, and Israfel wants to hate him for it. But he knows that he has to confront these things eventually, that Michael, in many ways, has always been his conscience.

It's just... he isn't ready, and the thought makes him so tired.

He takes a deep breath, and with a monumental effort, shoves the concern down, down into the depths of himself. He can feel it there like an ache, like something gnawing, but at least it's contained. He turns to Nate. "Just... behave yourself, all right?" He shakes his head. "We have to stop this. We should have stopped this weeks ago, like I said, but...."

And it's rising again, coiling out of its cage in dark spirals of fear. Israfel pauses, retakes control of himself. "But," he goes on, "we didn't. So." He shrugs. "I suppose that's irrelevant, now. The point is that I don't want him running off to tell the Bishop, or the police. We can take the necessary action here ourselves, with God's help."

God has felt curiously reluctant to help when Israfel has asked before, but Israfel dismisses that thought as unworthy. Perhaps he has simply been unwilling to let himself be helped, up to this point. This will change. The thought of disappointing Michael yet again—

of disappointing his parents, of everything he's worked for lying in ruins around him—will surely spur him on.

He does not dwell on the fact that all of these considerations come from outside himself, outside of his own convictions.

"Hey," Nate says again, his voice still gentle. "Hey, I know. I'll be good, I promise. You want me to just slip out, make some excuse, I can."

"He wants you to stay," Israfel says, glumly. He rubs a hand across his mouth, a tired, abortive gesture. "Wants you to stay for dinner. Says his wife and daughter will like you. He wants to ask you about living in the parish, what it was like before, all that stuff." He hesitates a moment and then lets himself vent the thought that's been clouding the back of his mind for long minutes now. "I... I have a feeling he may suspect. I think he'd like to assure himself that you're just one of my young parishioners, and nothing else."

Nate frowns at Israfel sidelong. "Suspect? Why would he—"

"We're *twins*, Nate," Israfel retorts heavily. "He knows about... about me. Of course he knows." He snorts. "He's the one who first suggested the priesthood as the best way for me to stay out of damnation's way."

Nate looks, for a second, as if he's about to launch into some kind of irate tirade, but, to his great credit, he arrests himself in time. Perhaps he knows that Israfel isn't in a mood to listen to it right now. Perhaps he knows a lot about Israfel these days.

"I'll be good," he repeats stoically. "Look, I can pull off 'good son' same as anyone. Better, even. I can be a hell of an actor." He smiles, squeezes Israfel's shoulder. "I do it for my mother every day, don't I? Huh?"

Israfel laughs shortly, despite himself. "Yes, I-I suppose you do," he concedes.

"Right?" Nate says, encouraging. "So, why don't you just stop worrying and get your clothes on, and I'll go down and get things started. You need potatoes peeled?"

Sometimes, Israfel has to admit, Nate is a welcome surprise to him. It's in moments like these that Israfel has to see him for all of what he is: not just some sex-crazed adolescent, bent on indulging his taste for the unattainable with reckless abandon, but *Nate*, the altar server, the measured, intelligent young man who's taken care of his little brother for years while their parents were involved in one church function or another. In many ways, Nate is inherently trustworthy.

Israfel suspects that he has too much faith in Nate. It's easy, the way it's never been quite so easy to have faith in anything else.

He smiles, leans up to kiss Nate's cheek. It's more of a quietly affectionate gesture than he's used to giving, and he feels a little awkward afterward, as if Nate might protest the presumption. He moves on quickly. "Yes. Thank you. And then chop them up?"

"I can do mash," Nate assures him, turning his face to brush their mouths together. He seems, Israfel thinks nervously, unconcerned by Israfel's behavior. "And 'shiny church boy'. So, you,"—he nudges Israfel in the direction of the door—"clothes. I won't put a foot wrong, cross my heart."

Nate paints a cross in the air across his chest in earnest demonstration, and he looks so wide-eyed and sincere that Israfel can't help but laugh.

"Fine. Don't cut yourself!" he calls, as Nate starts off down the stairs.

All he gets in return is a wave of Nate's hand in acknowledgement, but it's enough. Israfel may have trouble with what's right these days, but he's beginning to feel that he's definitely right to trust Nate. Nate's a good kid.

What Israfel should *not* trust, it seems, is the intention of the universe toward one Father Israfel Vacek. It makes sense, of course. He is doing wrong, and He who hears the cadences of everything is only too aware of it. Michael is his conscience, here to hear his confession, even if that confession must be forced.

When Israfel comes downstairs ten minutes later, none of this has crossed his mind. His hair is dry and his blue shirt and dress pants are respectable enough to see family in, even if he really should be wearing his cassock. Nate is in the kitchen, peeling things in readiness for Israfel's arrival. If he's honest with himself, there's a delusional little part of him that's almost looking forward to the domesticity of it, of Nate helping him make dinner for his brother. It's stupid, but then, Israfel has been stupid over Nate from the start.

The kitchen has two doors. The house is quite an old one, and drafty, so there are doors everywhere, making pockets for warm air to collect in when winter comes. Israfel is just approaching the door into the kitchen from the hallway when he hears the low rumble of Nate's voice, warm and pleased. "*There* you are," he's saying, and the *snick-snick* of his knife on the chopping block stills.

Israfel stills, too, arrested at the door in a welter of incomprehension.

Then he hears Michael's voice, a laugh, perhaps a little bemused, and then, "Here I am indeed." Israfel knows that tone. It's the, 'where'd you think I was, Raf?' tone; the 'didn't realize you cared if I was here or not, Raf' tone, reminding him of those first awful years of their growing apart. The fact that Michael, in bemusement, sounds so similar to Israfel was just another twist of the knife in those days, the sameness casting their new differences in a harsh and unrepentant light.

Something goes cold in the region of Israfel's heart. Nate is talking to Michael. There is nothing wrong, inherently, with the idea of Nate talking to Michael. Indeed, Nate is here purely because Michael thought that talking to him would be a Good Thing. And Israfel doesn't think for a moment, not now, that Nate will do anything to condemn him. But there's something about the way Nate is talking to Michael that makes Israfel's muscles seize up nervously. It's *familiar*, he might say, and Nate has no reason to use that tone with Michael at all. The way Nate laughs back is the way he laughs when he's quietly amused by Israfel's hesitance, his moments of shy diffidence. It's not a sound Israfel's ever heard from him otherwise, and where he normally finds it reassuring, hearing it now makes the back of his neck prickle unhappily.

He's only just edged his way around the doorframe when he sees Nate moving, his body too far gone in the motion for Israfel to do anything to stop it. It's nothing obscene, nothing horrific, but the slight press of his body against Michael's, intended to comfort, and the way he leans up, hand cupping the nape of his neck, is a subtle seal of doom. Israfel has barely time to open his mouth in abject horror before Michael's twisting away, face contorting with fluster, and then Nate's hand is clamped over his own mouth in a gesture Israfel has only ever seen in movies.

Then, "Raf," Michael rasps out, and Nate spins to look at him, eyes wide with something still too full of disbelief to have progressed to apology. Not that it matters at this point.

Israfel's skin feels suddenly damp all over, sticky with cold sweat. It doesn't stop him smiling his little things-are-A-okay smile, if only for Nate's benefit, as he steps into the room and spreads his arms. Michael's taken off the coat he was wearing earlier, leaving him in a pale blue shirt very similar to the one Israfel is wearing. For two such very different characters, their twin instinct always did seem to show through in their shared taste in clothes.

"Nice shirt," Israfel says breezily, although the edges of his voice shake. "How're those potatoes, Nate?"

He isn't sure when exactly he decided that bluffing was the only way to go here. Possibly it was a decision made by his subconscious in a moment of blackness induced by the realization. At any rate, it's the only plan he's got, so it seems foolhardy to reject it.

He can practically *see* the elephant looming large and apoplectic by the sink, somewhere in the vicinity of Nate. The curious thing about large elephants in small rooms, though, is that people tend strangely to follow each other's lead on how best to behave toward them, and Nate, sure enough, after a moment's blank confusion, stumbles out a reply. "Most of 'em are done, I think,

Padre." He clears his throat and indicates the piles of cubed potato on the chopping board. "Unless you think we'll need more?"

"Should be enough," Israfel says, after a cursory glance. His own voice sounds alien, uncharacteristically strident and brisk. He can still feel Michael's eyes on him, and he looks up, emboldened by anxiety, holds his gaze. "Unless you and the girls are particularly ravenous, Michael?"

There's a moment's hesitation, and Israfel feels his heart pounding in his throat. But then Michael's brow unclouds a little, and the pounding lessens a little when he speaks. "No, I-I think we're good. They're still in the car. I brought it around the back to park it." He indicates with a jab of his thumb. "And then thought I'd better pop back in to make sure you were decent before I let in the hordes. The back door was open; hope you don't mind."

He shrugs, shoves his hands into the pockets of his slacks. His face is still uncertain, his mouth a tight line when he's done speaking, but his eyes are wider, processing. Doubting his own assumptions, Israfel hopes and prays, because of the sheer force of Israfel's bluster.

"Not at all," Israfel tells him. He can't even remember the last time he used the back door, so it is a little unnerving to be informed that it may have been standing unlocked for days. But then, this is just that sort of village. People don't even lock their doors at night here.

Israfel spreads his arms a little, shrugging. "I'm ready for them. I didn't cassock up, but...."

Michael, to Israfel's great relief, smiles a little at that, waving a hand dismissively. "Never mind that. Claire might be a little disappointed not to have seen Uncle Raf's 'dress', but I think I can live with the breach of decorum." He hesitates for a second and then takes a step forward, bypassing Nate and holding out an arm. "Two years is too long."

Israfel knows Michael's face better than he knows his own, and he knows Michael is still dubious. But he accepts the gesture for what it is, stepping gratefully forward into his brother's outstretched arm. Michael is, of course, far too grown up a man to hug his brother properly any more, preferring a sort of one-armed combination of spine-breaking squeeze and thump to the back of the lung. It is, frankly, more painful than comforting—Israfel misses the perfect symmetry of their childhood embraces, how comfortable it felt to grip each other tight—but if this is Michael's gesture of greeting now, then Israfel must fall in line with it.

Michael steps back after a second and turns toward the door he entered by. The house is a warren of corridors and curiously shaped rooms, with the back door leading onto a little hallway that opens into the living room, which, in its turn, opens onto both the front hallway and the kitchen. Israfel has never been so exasperated with the architect as he is in this moment.

He turns to Nate the moment he hears the back door slam. "Did you—"

"I thought he was you," Nate blurts, his voice overloud with insistence. "I didn't think he was back in the house. I didn't even know there *was* a back door."

Israfel hushes him, and the sound is harsh in the quiet of the kitchen. "I know. Believe me, I realize that." He takes a breath, passes a hand over his face. Now that Michael is gone, all the bravado has dropped out of his voice, leaving it thready and trembling with aftershock.

"I thought you'd just gone round through the living room to straighten up or something," Nate goes on fumblingly. There's a hint of defiance in his voice that suggests he's attempting to ward off a punishment, and Israfel puts up a hand, stops him with a hand on his shoulder.

"All right," he says, sharply. "All right. Believe me, Nate, I don't think you were deliberately hitting on my brother." He shakes his head, and then, because it's niggling at the back of his mind and he's too on edge not to say it, he adds, "Although even if he *had* been me, I don't think touching me in the kitchen would have been the best plan with them due to arrive any second, do you?"

"It wasn't like I shoved him up against the counter and had my wicked way with him!" Nate raps out, defensively. "It was just—"

"Reassurance," Raf supplies, and sighs. "I know. It's just...." He shrugs. "I may have put him off exploding about it, but I think I'll be more than lucky if he lets it go entirely." He pulls open the freezer door with undue force and starts tossing out fillets of salmon onto a baking tray. The sound they make as they connect with the metal is unduly satisfying. "Frankly," he goes on, reaching for the olive oil, "I think it'll be a fucking miracle. Not that I deserve one."

Nate flinches visibly at the sound of the unfamiliar curse word as it passes Israfel's lips. Israfel knows that he shouldn't find the shocked little jerk in any way satisfying, but Israfel is not feeling quite himself just now. He shoves the baking tray into the oven and flips on the heat rather aggressively. Nate heaves an uncertain little breath.

"Raf—"

"Just behave," Israfel says, cutting him off. "All right? I know it's not... I know this is not, God help me, your responsibility to conceal or defend, but *please*. For me. Be as formal as you can, and as polite as you can, and"—he flips his fingers, thinking—"act like you're interested in classics or something. Dead languages or church history, *something*."

"Lie," Nate translates, and the curt truth of it makes Israfel's stomach twist.

"Nate," he says, on a low, warning note.

"I know," Nate says heavily. He leans into a cupboard for a pan, pulls off the lid and starts tossing the chopped potatoes haphazardly into it. "Don't worry about it. I'll do it. It's just...." He shrugs. "Don't you ever get tired of lying all the damn time, Raf?"

Israfel frowns. "Well, I wouldn't have to, would I? If it hadn't been for you, and—and *this*, and—"

Nate slams the pan down hard on the countertop, hard enough that Israfel starts. Nate's eyes are bright, bright green, but the burn in them isn't one Israfel has seen there for a long time, not since the first time Nate spat accusations at him and then stormed off into the night. Israfel is suddenly awash with trepidation. Nate *can't* storm off, not if he wants even a chance at covering this up.

"Nate," he says more reasonably, attempting to forestall any explosion before it happens.

It seems to have little effect. Nate's drawn himself up to say his piece, and he clearly intends to do so.

"You wouldn't have to lie about *fucking* me, maybe," he spits, "but that's not exactly all that's going on, is it? I didn't make you gay, Raf. You've been lying about that for a long fucking time, far as I can see." He shoves the pan aggressively under the faucet, turns it on full. "It's not even like I went out of my way to make you want me, Jesus. You weren't exactly subtle."

It's true. All of it is so much unwanted truth, tripping out of Nate's mouth like it isn't something Israfel has kept unspoken, holed up in his silence for years. He closes his eyes. "I know," he says, quietly. "I know, Nate. And like I said, this is not your responsibility, but—"

"I just don't see how you could want to live like that," Nate says shortly. He turns on the ring and transfers the pan to it, slamming on the lid rather fiercely.

"Nate—" Israfel starts, but Nate waves a hand, shaking his head.

"I'll play your stupid role for you, *Father*. Don't worry. I just...." He shrugs. "I don't think you realize what a liar you are, you know? I don't see how it makes you a better person spiritually when all you ever do is bear false witness."

The clatter of the back door jolting open saves Israfel—graciously, mercifully—from having to summon an answer to a question he has long suppressed, simply because he *has* no response to it. Nate frowns a little, as if annoyed by the interruption, but there are voices approaching, and then the sound of small footsteps, moving in haste.

"Claire?" Israfel calls out, voice hesitating on the edge of a smile. "Is that my favorite niece I hear?"

Sure enough, the next second the door is hurtling open under the impact of sixty pounds of eight-year-old girl. "Uncle Raf!" she yells, before barrelling headlong toward Israfel's shins.

It may have been two years, but Israfel is ready. He laughs despite himself, catches her under the armpits and swings her up neatly onto his hip. "Hey, sweetheart. Did you miss me or something?"

Claire's arms go around his neck immediately, small and strong and clinging. Israfel smiles at her, leans across to kiss her cheek.

"She's been hyperactive since the moment we suggested visiting," comes a woman's voice from the doorway. Israfel looks up to see Charlotte, with Michael hovering behind her.

"Well," Israfel says, "I'm very happy to see you all. How are you, Charlotte?" He crosses the room, Claire held tightly on his hip, and leans up to kiss Charlotte politely on the ridge of her cheekbone. "I'd ask you in, but…." He gestures. "It's kind of a small kitchen."

"It's nice," Charlotte says, smiling. "And really, don't worry about it. I'm sure we can wait out here." She curls her fingers in the crook of Michael's arm. "Can't we, honey?"

"Sure," Michael says, in a voice that reveals nothing. "Claire?"

"I wanna stay here," Claire protests immediately, and her little arms tighten. Israfel shrugs.

"She can stay if she likes," he assures his brother. "She'll be no trouble. Will you, Claire?"

Claire shakes her head vehemently. "Want to stay here with Uncle Raf and that boy," she reiterates.

Nate laughs, and Israfel starts at the sound of it. He'd sort of blocked out, for a minute, the fact of Nate's presence in the kitchen. It made things easier. But now Nate is leaning over to shake Claire's hand, and then crossing to the door to repeat the gesture for Charlotte's sake. "Nate Mulligan," he explains. "I'm a protégé of Father Israfel's."

By the look on Charlotte's face, Israfel can see that she's impressed, and something in his chest sags with relief. If he can be sure that Michael hasn't said anything to his wife, it may relieve at least *some* of the tension over the dinner table.

"Protégé?" she says, looking between Nate and Israfel. "Are you considering the priesthood, too, Nate?"

Nate shrugs, smiling the charming smile he reserves for elderly ladies at bake sales. "Possibly. Something like that."

"Well," Charlotte says, as she withdraws her hand, "you couldn't wish for a better guide than Raf, here. I think I'm safe in saying he's the most intelligent person I've ever met."

"Charlotte," Israfel protests, while his insides writhe guiltily.

"He's modest, too," Charlotte says, tipping Nate a little wink. "Anyway, we'll leave you to it. We can talk more later. There's a lot of catching up to be done, isn't there, Raf?"

Israfel can feel himself blushing and curses his fair skin, not for the first time in recent weeks. "Out of my kitchen," he orders with feigned firmness, and the door closes on Charlotte's laugh. Michael's silence is uncharacteristic, and it tugs at Israfel a little, but it isn't as if he hadn't expected it. He sighs and sets Claire down on the floor.

Any concerns he may have felt about Claire and her particular interest in Nate are swiftly dispelled by the way their interaction makes the atmosphere in the little kitchen bearable. Nate's good with children—has proven himself so on many occasions, to Israfel's knowledge—and Claire is swiftly besotted with him. Israfel works around them, taking the potatoes off the boil when necessary, draining and mashing and seasoning while Nate crouches on the floor and tells Claire about being home-schooled. He sounds so sweetly earnest that, for a moment, Israfel can almost forget about their argument in the wake of his urge to lean down and ruffle Nate's hair, to kiss him in passing, just as an outlet for this rush of affection.

This is why Israfel is utterly fucked.

He shakes his head to clear it and begins setting out the salmon and (bagged) salad on plates. The potatoes he spoons into a large glass bowl that very rarely gets any use, for people to dispense as they wish. "Nate," he says flatly, as he works, "do you think you could lay the table for me?"

When he emerges with the first two plates, he finds the dining room table immaculately set, cutlery and place mats and glasses all exactly where they should be. Nate holds Israfel's eyes as he passes him, walking back toward the kitchen, but his expression is veiled. Israfel is just about to turn around and go back for the other three plates when Nate re-enters the room with them in hand, one balanced expertly in the crook of his elbow.

"Mom gives a lot of dinner parties," Nate explains, in response to Israfel's raised eyebrow. He shrugs. "No big deal." He looks down at Claire, now tripping happily across the floor to take up a position by Nate's knee. "You want to go get your parents, babe?"

The "babe" works like some kind of magic word. Claire glows with pleasure, skipping off obediently in the direction of the living room. When she returns, Michael and Charlotte in tow, Nate and Israfel are standing awkwardly behind their chairs, and Israfel is glad for her small voice in the uncomfortable silence.

Throughout the meal, Michael continues to be uncommunicative. It has generally fallen upon Israfel to say grace at family gatherings ever since he entered the seminary, and Michael dutifully ducks his head as they all hold hands around the table, says a firm "Amen." After this, though, he is quiet—contemplative, Israfel thinks. It's possible, of course, that he's reading too much into it. Nate is talking quite animatedly to Charlotte, providing a highly detailed picture of life in the parish, and Michael does look mildly interested. But his contributions to the conversation are few and far between, consisting mostly of remarks like, "And you've served altar for a while, then?" and, "So, Raf says you have a keen interest in the Church?" They're unashamedly probing questions, questions specifically about Nate, and Israfel doesn't like it.

Israfel, for his own part, barely speaks at all. He answers Charlotte's questions about how he's enjoying the parish ("It's very friendly.") and his feelings on Latin Mass ("You know I've always been a fan of Latin."). Mostly, though, he only watches anxiously as the others converse, the thread of concern in his stomach winding tighter as the time goes on.

There's a Scrabble set in the front room, and Claire has been agitating to play with it since she gave up on her potatoes halfway through the meal. Eventually, when everyone else's plate is empty, Charlotte takes pity on her daughter, whose exuberance has now transmuted itself into the slump of the disengaged child.

"Okay, Claire," she says, with a little smile. "Why don't you ask Uncle Raf if you can leave the table, and maybe we'll go play Scrabble, huh?"

Claire perks up immediately. "Oh! Yes!" She bounces in her chair. "Uncle Raf, pleasemayIleavethetable?" She widens her eyes earnestly. "I want to play Scrabble with Mom." Her eyes slide sideways as she smiles. "And Nate."

Nate laughs. "You really want me to play? I'm not that great at it, you know."

Israfel snorts. "You're an awful lot cleverer than you pretend to be, Nate," he says, because he can't stop himself and doesn't really feel like trying. "Yes, Claire, you can leave the table. Go on, go show your Mom how smart you are. There's a bowl of M&Ms on the coffee table out there, if you're interested."

Claire's speedy departure, Israfel thinks, seems to answer his question quite effectively. Nate stands up more slowly, holding

Israfel's eye as he follows Claire and her mother to the door. "You coming?" he asks, his voice low and unreadable.

Israfel has barely opened his mouth to reply before Michael cuts in. "In a minute, Nate. Close the door behind you, would you?"

The pit of Israfel's stomach plummets immediately into his socks. When he stands, he half expects Michael to snap at him to take his seat again, but he doesn't. Instead, he walks slowly around the table until he can curl a hand around Israfel's arm, and the ominous deliberateness of it is far worse than any harsh words of command could have been.

"Come here," Michael says softly, at the lowest pitch of his voice. "I need to talk to you a minute."

Fourteen

ISRAFEL lets himself be guided across to the far side of the room, over to the corner that marks the furthest point from the living room. There is really, he thinks, numbly, very little else that he can do. Michael's mouth is set, and there's no resisting Michael when he looks like that.

"So," Michael says, slipping his hands casually into his pockets. "Are you going to deal with this yourself, or do I need to tell the Bishop?"

All the blood in Israfel's body seems to rush to his stomach, churning there in hideous roils of heat. "What?"

It's a last-ditch attempt at deception, and he knows it's a poor one. The heat in his stomach may have diverted the blood from his face, but he can *feel* how white he must look, and that is hardly better. His voice cracks agonizingly over his exclamation.

Michael, sure enough, is not taken in. He snorts, withdrawing his hands and crossing them pointedly across his chest. "You *know* what, Raf. I thought we dealt with this."

Israfel's pulse is sprinting in his gut, throbbing there like nausea. "Dealt with what?" he hazards, although he knows it's useless. "Michael, I don't know what you're—"

"I'm talking about you sodomizing that boy!" Michael rasps out, abrupt and fierce, and his face is suddenly only inches from Israfel's own.

Shame rises up in Israfel like a flood, hearing those words spoken aloud. He ducks his head, feeling the heat darken his cheeks at last. "I haven't," he says, weakly. "Michael, I don't—"

"Then you're close to it," Michael retorts, unrelenting. "I'm not an idiot, Raf. I know you. And I know you have a problem with this, but honestly, wasn't that the point of"—he spreads his arms to encompass the rectory, the crucifix on the wall—"all *this*? You're going to burn in hell if you go on like this. You know that. It's not exactly better now that you've made a vow of celibacy, is it?"

Israfel takes a step back, suddenly desperate for air. He presses his hand to his flaming cheek, and breathes, and breathes. The situation as it stands seems curiously unreal, impossible in its horror. He shakes his head meaninglessly. "I don't know why—" he starts, but Michael cuts him off with a hand under his chin, jerking his face upward.

"Don't give me that. The kid went to kiss me, Raf. He thought I was you. Which means he thought you wouldn't mind, and there's only one reason he could possibly have for making that kind of assumption about his priest."

There's a beat, in which Israfel can do nothing but stare, eyes wide and unblinking. Then, like a light going out, the harshness flickers out of Michael's gaze, to be replaced by something closer to pity, a sort of pleading earnestness.

"*Raf.* Look, I'm telling you this because I care about you. God knows I could have gone straight to the Bishop and had you defrocked, but I don't want to do that. I know it's not... your fault, exactly. You're sick, and they probably wouldn't understand that. I don't want you to end up in prison. And I know you're a good priest." He sighs. "But you need to stop this, Raf. You're condemning him, and you're condemning yourself. If you weren't, oh, ten years older than him—and his priest—it'd be bad enough, but as it is, there's only one way it can end." He breaks off, breathing heavily with effort. "Unless you end it now. That's the only chance there is. End it now, and then pray like you've never prayed before for this burden to be lifted from you."

"It won't be," Israfel says in a voice he hardly recognizes. The words are soft, almost whispered, and they're out of his mouth before he's had a chance to think. "It won't be lifted from me, Michael. I've been asking for that for, what, fifteen years, now? And—"

"It's your *trial*," Michael hisses, taking hold of Israfel's shoulders. "It's your trial. You know that. We've talked about this." He exhales, slow, as if he's trying to steady himself. "God knows I'd rather you didn't have to deal with this. I love you. I wish you could be normal, just...." He flails his hands in agitation. "You know, have a wife and kids, come over to our house for dinner on Sundays, go to the park. Be my brother. But God didn't see fit to give that to you, Raf, and there has to be a reason for that. You have to work with what you've got."

Every word out of Michael's mouth seems to ram a little further home into Israfel's chest. His body aches from the inside out, behind his heart, behind his eyes. He reaches up, pressing both hands to his temples, as if that might relieve some of the pressure. "And what the hell have I got, Michael?" he demands. "I've got something inside of me that it takes all my effort to control. You have no idea what it's like, carrying that... that *evil* around, like it wants to control you, and—"

"And you can control *it!*" Michael's eyes are blazing, his fingers pressing bruises into Israfel's upper arms. "You can, Raf. You're stronger than this. That's why you were given this burden to shoulder, so you could prove yourself." He leans in, presses his forehead to Israfel's, and Israfel lets himself lean into it, lets his eyes fall closed.

"Stop this," Michael whispers, so close that Israfel can feel the warmth of his breath. "Will you stop it, for me? If I promise, God forgive me, not to let it go beyond this room?"

Up close like this, Michael's earnestness is catching, like some kind of airborne disease. It's always had this effect on Israfel, for as long as he can remember. Michael may profess a belief in Israfel's strength, but Israfel knows that Michael is the strong one, the effortless controller of destinies. Michael wants to believe in him, and Israfel so wants Michael's faith to be justified.

And then there is the fact that Michael is perfectly right about the many hells Israfel would suffer for this, if he were to let it go on. The Bishop, and potentially a judge, would surely put him through hell on earth, only for the same fate to greet him, redoubled, at the end of things.

Michael is right. Israfel has no desire to meet such a fate.

"All right," he says, softly. "I'll stop it, Michael. I promise you." He breathes out, and his breath is faint and shaky. "Thank you. You didn't have to—"

"You're my brother," Michael says, pulling him in for another brief celebratory backslap. "I have to give you a chance, don't I?" He smiles, a very little smile, but a smile nonetheless. "I believe in you."

Israfel smiles back, a weak, feathery little thing, but meant. "Thank you," he says again. "Really."

The evening, after that, is long and strange. The five of them play three games of Scrabble, all of which are won resoundingly by Nate. Israfel is not really paying attention, and he knows Michael isn't, either. All he can think about is the curve of Nate's lower lip, the shine on his teeth when he smiles. His soft hair, and his soft skin, and the fact that Israfel must never touch either again.

For a long, long time, Israfel got by on such small indulgences as these stolen glances.

The Vaceks leave a little before nine o'clock, Claire smothering both Nate and Israfel in hugs as her mother hauls her, laughing, through the door. Michael is last to leave, pausing to grip Israfel's shoulder as he passes, the wordless gesture perfectly clear.

It is meant for fortification, but as he stands in his empty living room with Nate, Israfel doesn't feel fortified at all.

For a long, long moment, neither of them speaks. The sound of the door closing behind Michael seems to resonate in the room, thunderously final. Israfel draws a deep breath, and thinks very hard about the Bishop.

"Nate," he begins. He has no concept of what he intends to say next, but it seems like a good beginning.

Nate appears to disagree. He collapses abruptly onto the couch and glares up at Israfel. "I hope you're about to thank me for all that dirty work I just fucking did for you," he says.

Israfel blinks a little, slightly thrown. He is grateful to Nate, of course, for keeping his promise, but he can't allow the conversation to be derailed. If it strays now, he will lose the momentum Michael gave him, and then... then he will never be able to do what he should.

Israfel isn't anything like as strong as Michael likes to believe he is.

"I am," he says slowly. "I mean, I will. Thank you. I'm grateful."

It's a preamble, for Israfel, something to be dealt with before he can move on, but Nate doesn't seem to see it that way. He's snapping back before Israfel has had a chance to gather his thoughts, let alone say his main piece.

"You better be," Nate says, and his voice is sharp and shattered, broken glass. "You better be, Raf, because I may be many questionable things, but I'm no fucking liar. And I just lied my pretty little ass off for you, there, for hours. So don't you look at me like you're gonna launch some kind of attack, Padre. Don't you *dare*."

The timbre of Nate's voice is not one Israfel has ever heard there before. He swallows hard against the uneasy rumble of his pulse. "I wasn't going to attack you," he says carefully. "Nate, it's just that… tonight brought home to me more than ever that—"

"You know what tonight brought home to *me*?" Nate interjects fiercely.

Israfel doesn't, but he doesn't seem to have any choice in whether or not he wishes to find out.

"What this whole fucking charade brought home to me," Nate goes on, "is that you are nothing, *nothing*, but a pansy-ass coward, Israfel. You fucking *know* what you are, and you know you can't change it. And you should know, Jesus *fucking* Christ, that the way you're made is the way you're meant to be."

Israfel takes a breath, but it never makes it out of his mouth. Nate's barrelling on far too quickly for that.

"But you can't accept that, can you?" Nate's lip curls up in something like a sneer. "You're just too *fucking* closed-minded to actually listen to the way things are, for once, instead of just believing the shit everyone else tells you about how they should be. And you lie, and you judge, and you spin out your scared little hypocritical agenda every day of your life, the way you always *fucking* have."

He's breathing hard now, chest rising and falling with his words, and his eyes are bright-burnished.

"Nate," Israfel breaks in, although his throat is full of blind, blank panic, Nate's tirade only ratcheting it higher. "Look, you're right, okay? You're right. I'm a hypocrite, and I'm sorry, but this is going to be the end of it."

"Damn *right* it's gonna be the end of it," Nate retorts, swift and sharp. "Because you know what else I realized, Israfel? I don't want to be like you, okay? I'm not gonna toe your fucking party line and lie about what I do, what I *am*. There's nothing *fucking* wrong with it and I'm not gonna spend another second with someone who thinks that there is, someone who's ashamed of me."

He stands, and Israfel is reminded all over again of just how tall Nate actually is, of how imposing he can be.

"I am nothing," he raps out, "to be ashamed of. I am fucking worth being with, and I'm not gonna spend another second with someone who thinks otherwise. Which, you know, I *really* wish you'd just get the fuck over yourself, Raf, I do, but...." He throws out his hands in surrender, in a gesture of helplessness. "You're not gonna. And I think I just realized that."

Nate's at the front door in a matter of seconds, out of it in a couple more, and Israfel is...

Israfel *is*. Whole beats go by while he stares blankly at the door, at the space where Nate was. He could swear that, ten minutes ago, he'd been about to break off a casual sexual entanglement with a boy he should never have touched, save both their souls and repent his own stupidity in loving at his leisure. And now, inexplicably, he is left with the impression that Nate has just stormed away from an affair Israfel was unaware that they were having. Nate just yelled blue murder at him about the impossibility of the two of them remaining together, when Israfel had never been quite stupid enough to think... to *assume*....

His eyes burn, a headache pounding through his skull behind them. The dining room is a mess, but the inside of Israfel's head is a worse one. He had it all planned, how this conversation was going to go. He was going to tell Nate, calmly and firmly, that he'd been wrong to go along with this whole stupid thing, that he's sorry, and he repents. He was going to advise him to find some other church in which to confess. To pour out his heart and pray to God that he might be forgiven. And then Israfel would have prostrated himself before the altar, as priests did in the olden days, and begged, and begged. Indulgence of the flesh, for flesh's sake, is a great sin, and he had thought them guilty of it.

Now… now he doesn't know what to do. Nate preempted him, ended something, but Israfel isn't sure what it was. Nate raked up sins Israfel had barely even allowed himself to consider and dredged up something else Israfel can't stand to let himself think about.

If this was more than sex to Nate, as it is so much more than sex for Israfel, he doesn't know that he'll ever be able to move beyond it as he should.

He stops himself mid-thought, on the edge of dangerous ground. His head is throbbing, and the mess in the dining room isn't something he can cope with at the moment. The bed upstairs is made, sheets cleaned, but still, it will smell of Nate, his shampoo and the particular scent of his skin, and Israfel… *can't.*

As a seminarian, Israfel always had particular trouble sleeping during exam periods. Anxiety attacks have always been one of his failings, usually coupled with bouts of insomnia. At the seminary, Israfel's priest assured him that this was quite normal and that the doctor ought to be able to "give him something" for it.

What remains of the sleeping pills are still, Israfel knows, in the drawer of the sideboard. Without pausing to think about it, he pops out three, knocks them back with the remains of a glass of orange juice still standing on the dining room table.

He barely makes it to his bed before sleep, in its beneficence, starts to dull his senses. If the pillow beneath his cheek still smells of Nate, Israfel hasn't the wherewithal to tell.

It isn't, he knows, a long-term solution, but for now, it's the only one he's got.

Fifteen

FOR the next several days, Israfel sticks to the short-term solution. He isn't exactly sure at what point the descriptor "short-term" will cease to be applicable, but hopefully the situation will have resolved itself by then.

So far, though, this outcome is looking fairly unlikely.

Israfel has never been much for complicated resolutions. He's written—and delivered—enough papers on determinism and fate and free will to know that, although a man may fuck up royally all on his own *within* the bus, the driver will ultimately get him to the same terminal, in whatever condition he may arrive. The Grand Plan, fate, is down to God, and no amount of prayer will change it. Israfel's homosexuality—though the word still makes his throat tense—is fated. The lesser things, though—the little acts of free will that make twists and loops in the path of a man's life—these are not predetermined. Israfel's hands on Nate, his mouth on all that bare skin—these were only bumps in the road, and prayer can bring a man safely back onto smooth ground.

So Israfel prays like the devil's at his back. He prays like a Jesuit, undertakes the Spiritual Exercises of St. Ignatius as he's never done in his whole active ministry. The exercises are in no way obligatory for Roman Catholic clergy, but Israfel feels that he has dire need of them just now. The primary aim of the Exercises, after all, is to develop "discernment," the ability to act upon one's spiritual training in what is right, to move with the Grace of God. Israfel knows, has always known, what is right, and yet has willingly done wrong, his own discipline insufficient to keep him from his sin. Discernment, *discretio*, is an attempt to forge a direct connection between the Grace of God and the supplicant's thought and action, to emphasize the mystical experience of faith. As Israfel's faith has proven too weak to withstand the onslaught of temptation, perhaps divine reinforcement is exactly what it needs.

Four days of exercises, and Israfel still dreams of Nate. He wakes at midnight, sticky; fumbles for his rosary and prays the Hail Mary until sleep pulls him back into oblivion, leaving his ejaculate to coagulate on his skin in self-abasement. Something more must be done.

He writes out his confession by hand, filling sheets upon sheets of paper. The point of confession, he reasons, is to have one's sins forgiven by God, for whom a priest is simply an intermediary. So confessing directly, without a middleman, should surely be enough?

He declaims his confession aloud in the middle of his living room, one hand cradling his crucifix. Between glances at his notes, he looks up at the icon of the Mother and Child that hangs above the low bookcase, eyes wide with sincerity.

"Please, Father, take this cup from me," he pleads. "If I am to overcome my inclinations, then I can do it, I *will* do it. But please, I don't want to think about Nate any longer. For his sake, and for mine, take these feelings from me, if You want me to move beyond him."

That night, in his dreams, Nate lies in Israfel's arms, his fingers tracing reverent paths over the bones of Israfel's face. It's a warm dream, supportive—barely even sexual. He *wants* Nate, with him, like this, wants the unmistakable love in his eyes.

The happiness lasts a long moment after Israfel wakes up, until he remembers that happiness is not what he's been praying for.

That Sunday, Anne and Jessica serve the Mass. Israfel can't remember—can't even remember where he might go to check—whether it's actually their turn or not. All he knows is that Nate isn't in the Mulligans' pew, and that this is somehow *more* of a distraction than it would have been to have to work around Nate and their implosion. This way, Nate just isn't here, and Israfel doesn't know why. His mind supplies a thousand possible reasons, each more unsettling than the last, as he stumbles through his homily. It doesn't help, either, that Tom is watching him steadily throughout the entirety of the Mass, almost as if he knows something.

This isn't exactly what Israfel had in mind when he envisaged a new, divinely abetted start.

Afterward, as he hears the confessions of the penitents, he feels unworthy, hypocritical—feels every one of the words Nate flung at him. It is true, he thinks, that the penitent's confession is a confession, ultimately, to God, but there is a reason that the Sacrament of Reconciliation exists, rather than the duty being left simply to the consciences of the faithful. Israfel has confessed to God, but these people have endured the far more immediate agony of confessing their wrongdoing to a real person, to a man behind a grille, whose minute reactions, catches of breath, are fully detectable to them. God's judgments are altogether more delayed, more distant, for all that He will make the ultimate call. It is far harder to make a confession to a priest—to form the words of one's sin aloud to a human being who, however schooled he may be in discretion, will nevertheless pass some judgment of his own. Israfel's trespasses have been greater than many, and the act of confession will be correspondingly more difficult. It is for this reason exactly, Israfel decides, that God requires this further trial from him, unsatisfied with his private contrition.

When the last penitent has left, then, and the church is an empty cavern around him, Israfel leaves. Leaves the church, leaves the rectory, gets in his car and leaves the little backwater town behind. There isn't much of anything around these parts, and there are many miles of nothing yawning ahead of Israfel, long after the town has disappeared from his rearview mirror. If one drives for long enough, though, one must come to some kind of settlement, and Israfel knows that there are at least one or two small towns between his own parish and the nearest big city. After almost an hour of pushing his little car as hard as he feels safe in doing, he comes to the first of these.

A peeling sign on the side of the road welcomes him to Portsmouth. It's a sleepy little place with a population of maybe five thousand people, neither a port nor the mouth of any river. It isn't remarkable to Israfel in any way, except in that it has a sizable Roman Catholic Church, whose service, apparently, is only now ending.

Israfel pulls over immediately. There aren't any lines on the road saying that it's okay to park here, but then, there aren't any lines saying that it isn't, and Israfel is feeling more than a little reckless. The outgoing parishioners seem slightly surprised to see an unfamiliar priest burrowing through the crowd, attempting to get *into* the church as they all pour out of it, but Israfel's cassock protects him, even while it excites their curiosity, and they let him by. The parishioners standing in the short line for the confessional seem still more interested in his presence among them, but Israfel is too relieved to find confession still going on to pay them much mind. His heart is pounding a frantic tattoo in his throat, in his gut, everywhere. Because the fact that this is going to happen now is terrifying, and yet, he is overwhelmingly grateful for it. Say his piece, make his confession, and perhaps he will be able to go on. Perhaps his prayers for aid will be, at last, answered.

Nobody joins the line behind Israfel, so that when he finally enters the booth, he is entirely alone with the priest. It is for him to speak first: "Forgive me, Father, for I have sinned." He is ludicrously, heart-racingly glad to hear an unfamiliar voice ask him, in response, how long it has been since his last confession. Had the voice belonged to someone he knew or recognized—someone from the seminary, or a priest he had spoken to at a conference—it would all have been so much more difficult, and it will be difficult enough as it is. Like this, though, it is truly anonymous, and Israfel takes what strength he can from that fact.

He makes a full confession. It isn't necessary, technically, for the penitent to explain his sins fully, provided that he is aware of where he has erred, but Israfel isn't taking any chances. He's driven an hour to get here, and his whole body is trembling with effort when he starts to speak, and a half-formed effort would be no better than the cheat he attempted—with the best intentions—in his own living room. So, he confesses. He explains, firstly, that he is a priest and that he has broken the discipline of celibacy. He explains that he has broken his vow on a number of occasions, and that the person who has been his partner in all these sins is a member of his congregation. Throughout all of this, the priest beyond the grille sits silent, unresponsive and patient.

Israfel explains that he has no intention of committing these sins again, but that it is proving more difficult than it should, perhaps, because he has fallen in love. He tells the priest that the man he loves is called Nate.

The priest, having valiantly kept his silence for so long, slips then, his breath coming out sharply in a hitch of surprise. Israfel silently thanks the Lord for his determination that "man," and not "boy," might be the safest term to use, for he has no doubt that his confessor's reaction, humbling though Israfel finds it, could have been far worse.

It is the priest's duty to advise, where he sees fit, and Israfel is entirely unsurprised by the advice he receives. His confessor urges him to tell the Bishop, to leave the priesthood. He tells Israfel that he has sullied himself, that he is no longer a pure man of the cloth.

Israfel argues. He tells the priest that he seeks forgiveness for his errors, that he will never commit them again. He points out that there have been many cases of priests entering the priesthood after a period of marriage, and that, provided that they promise celibacy during their ministry, a priest is not required to be a virgin.

It is on the tip of his tongue to point out, further, that he is still, actually, a virgin himself, but a twist of guilt at the nape of his neck stops the words in his mouth. While, technically, this would be true, it isn't true pragmatically, and Israfel knows it. Confessing openly like this, in an attempt to save his sanity and his career, it's probably best not to get caught up in technicalities.

The priest, to his credit, listens patiently to Israfel's contentions. He would not break the privileges of the confessional, this Israfel knows, and he does not attempt to force his suggestions upon Israfel, although he emphasizes that he feels a departure from the priesthood would be best.

"I don't want to leave," Israfel tells him, firmly. "I'm a good priest. I help people. I *guide* people, and I know I'm not perfect, but we are none of us perfect, are we, Father?" He sighs. "I have sinned terribly, I know. But I'm young, and I was tempted, and I failed. All I ask for is a second chance to prove myself. That's what God would want."

"You believe that?" the priest asks him cautiously, and Israfel answers him with a firm "yes."

If a small voice in his mind tells him that God has not really spoken here, so much as Michael has, Israfel ignores it.

After that, the priest makes no further attempts to advise. He sets penances instead, prayers and good deeds, has Israfel say the Act of Contrition aloud, and Israfel is pathetically grateful for the lack of judgment in his voice. He absolves Israfel in the name of the Father, the Son, and the Holy Spirit. Afterward, though, Israfel can hear him hesitating on the edge of something else, and he cannot hold back his prompting. "Father?"

The priest shifts a little, uncertainly. Israfel hears the creak of the bench under him as he moves. "I know we've spoken about this, my son, and I know it isn't what you think you want. But... sometimes, you know, people find that they're just not temperamentally suited to the priesthood. St. Paul himself said that not every man can be celibate. There's no shame in realizing that this life is not for you."

Israfel laughs. He doesn't intend to, but at the invocation of St. Paul, he cannot help himself. "For most people, Father, perhaps. But you forget: for all my best efforts, I'm still a homosexual."

The priest sighs, and Israfel hears in his voice, in the weariness of it, that he is old, a fact that evaded him until now. "I do not forget, my son," says the priest.

Israfel has nothing to say to that. His chest has clenched up again, and the priest's sudden tiredness seems to have sparked an answering lethargy in him, an exhaustion that starts in his bones. "May I go, Father?" he asks quietly.

The priest sighs again, something heavy and resigned in it this time. "Go in peace," he grants, after a moment.

"Thanks be to God," Israfel responds, and he leaves before his mind can run away with him, twisting the priest's words into a form he surely never intended.

The drive home seems shorter, now that the road is no longer unfamiliar territory, and Israfel is back at the rectory by midafternoon. He wants to feel free, unencumbered by the weight unloaded into the confessional booth in the sleepy little church, but there's still... *something*, niggling at the back of his mind, holding him back.

Israfel puts it down, uncertainly, to the fact that his penances are still outstanding. He makes himself some toast, with bread that has seen better days, and eats it mechanically, reciting the Hail Mary in his mind. Afterward, he takes out his rosary and carefully says his set prayers, letting each word sit in his mouth in a way that he hasn't for years. He prays each bead slowly, carefully, before moving on to the next. It takes a long time, like this, to get through the penance, but that, he supposes, is the point. He is supposed to *feel* it, to experience his contrition.

He feels a little better when he's done, goes upstairs to fetch his notepad, ready to start planning his first homily for the coming week. It comes easier, certainly, than it had the week before, and Israfel breathes deeply as he works, relieved.

Later, though, when the lights are out, and Israfel is staring blankly at the ceiling, he hears the priest's words, circling around his head unbidden. *Not every man can be celibate*, and, *I do not forget, my son.*

For untold minutes, he endures the remembrance stiffly, leaping upon every abortive attempt to delve into the priest's motivations before it can take proper form. Eventually—when it becomes clear that he will get no peace any other way—he retrieves his rosary beads from under his pillow and begins intoning the Our Father.

It's more prayers than were ordered in his penance, but more can't exactly do him any harm.

Sixteen

FOR the next three nights, all his dreams are of Nate. Israfel tries to tell himself that he should feel better, feel blessed, because they are not all dreams of Nate's filthy, perfect mouth and his hands, but it isn't true—somehow, it is worse this way. He dreams of Nate on his front on the living room carpet, laughing with Claire as he helps her with some massive-scoring word. Nate cuffing Tom around the head, the way he habitually does, and that look on his face that Israfel loves and loves and loves. Most of all, he dreams of Nate sitting with him, *being* with him, anywhere and everywhere—in Nate's car, in Israfel's kitchen, at the grocery store, and at the park. Nate's hand in his in the street somewhere, with the sun beating down yellow bright on the backs of their necks. Israfel dreams so much, he barely feels as if he's sleeping at all.

In all this time, he sees absolutely nothing of Nate. It's the longest he's gone without sight of Nate since the moment he moved here, and though he sees Lynda at one or two midweek services, Nate is not with her, nor is any mention made of him. Israfel wonders, nervously, what reason Nate has given her for not wishing to accompany her as he used to.

On Sunday, it is most definitely the Mulligans' turn to serve, and Israfel, treacherously, is looking forward to it. His chest feels strange and close, as if there is some sort of mechanism inside it winding tighter and tighter with every day that passes without Nate. It isn't that he means to impose upon Nate, nor have him go back on either of their promises. The decisions made, he knows, were for the best. But he loves Nate, for now. He can't help it, until the Lord has seen fit to help it for him. All these days without knowing Nate is even still here are beginning to wear on him from the inside.

He's rarely been so disappointed in his life as when he walks into the sacristy on Sunday morning to find Tom there alone, eyes affixed to his Game Boy.

"Hello, Tom," he says, but the question is clear in his voice, and the look on Tom's face, when he glances up at Israfel, is skeptical.

"Nate's sick," he says and turns back immediately to his Game Boy.

Israfel is more than a little hurt by the rebuff. He shouldn't be, he knows, because Tom is a thirteen-year-old boy, and thirteen-year-old boys are usually more interested in their Game Boys than in their priests. But Tom has never been that way with Israfel before. He remembers their first meeting, the way Tom turned the game off immediately in favor of speaking to him. He remembers all sorts of subsequent conversations, about literature and history and Nate.

Nate. Israfel can't help but feel uncomfortably as if he has something to do with this abrupt turnaround on Tom's part. Tom may have seemed fond of Israfel, but he is fiercely, *viscerally* devoted to Nate, a fact that is perfectly obvious despite their constant bickering and jibes at each other. If there is anything that might make a boy like Tom decide suddenly and with no warning to start treating Israfel like a mildly untrustworthy stranger, then it's surely some sense that he has done something to hurt his brother.

Israfel just wonders, anxiously, what Tom thinks the "something" is.

"He's sick?" Israfel says cautiously.

"He's been sick all week," Tom retorts icily. "He just sits in his room and won't talk to Mom and Dad."

"Will he talk to you?" Israfel asks, going for casual.

The look on Tom's face suggests strongly that he doesn't quite manage it. "Yes," Tom says, prim and enigmatic, and immediately falls silent.

Israfel is far from reassured. He shifts uneasily. "Well, I-I'm sorry to hear that. Send him my best wishes, won't you?"

Tom twists his mouth slightly in what Nate calls his "little bitch face." Israfel can almost hear him saying it, can almost see the way he'd laugh and coax Tom out of it, if he were here, and the thought makes him ache emptily. He hastens on.

"We'll do a more basic Mass, then, if you're on your own today. I'll take the missal out myself beforehand, if you just put the candles out first and then come ahead of me with the Cross, yes? And then just do Book."

Tom nods curtly, but his eyes are fixed stonily on the little matchbox screen of his console. His tongue pokes out in concentration. Israfel sighs and sits down carefully on a plastic chair, two along from Tom's.

"Tom," he says, gently, "are you unhappy with me?"

Tom hesitates a moment and then says, without looking up, "Nate's unhappy with you." He wrinkles his nose. "So, yes."

Israfel frowns, turning his crucifix nervously in his fingers. He tries to laugh, but it comes out as more of a pained little gasp. "If Nate jumped off a bridge, would you do that too?"

"Yes," Tom says stubbornly, defiantly, jabbing the buttons down hard. The Game Boy makes a series of little bleeping noises, *meep meep meep meep byaow*. "He'd pro'ly have a good reason for it."

The implication is perfectly clear, and Israfel sits back, understanding that he won't get anywhere with Tom in a mood like this. "Look," he says, reasonably, "I didn't *mean* to upset your brother—"

"Well, you did," Tom cuts in. The childish sing-song tone to his voice is absolutely at odds with the firmness of it, the unrelenting lack of apology.

"*Tom,*" Israfel says, exasperated. The open appeal in his voice somehow gets in there without his say-so, but something in it must move Tom, regardless, because he looks up, finally, lowers the Game Boy in his lap.

"Look," he says, tight little expression still firm on his face. "I don't know, exactly, what's happened, but I know it's something to do with you. Nate likes you. A *lot*. He was always over here. And then suddenly he's not, and he's just all messed up all the time. It doesn't take a genius to work out that you guys had a fight. And it must have been your fault, because if Nate upset *you*, he'd just be all swaggery and in denial about it, the way he gets." He shrugs and raises the console again. "So. I like you, Father, but right now you're just the guy who's got my brother all wound up and sad. I'm sure you understand."

This last comes out on a surge of spite of a sort Israfel has never heard from anyone so young, let alone from quiet, clever Tom. But the fact of it is that he *does* understand—understands Tom's motivations, at least, and can't really bring himself to blame him for them. Nate's motivations, on the other hand....

Israfel's head hurts. He stands up with a sigh, nodding resignedly to Tom. "All right," he says, "I understand that, Tom. And I am sorry."

Tom says nothing, just nods his head a little in acknowledgement. Israfel gives up and goes to make sure there's holy water in the stoup.

After that, things are palpably, horribly, harder. Before, Israfel had at least been able to assure himself that he was suffering alone, and that it was all for the best. He would suffer his dues, make his penances, and say his prayers, and in the end, both he and Nate would be better off. Knowing, though, that Nate is suffering, too, makes everything in him hurt. His whole world seems slewed to one side, as if all his assumptions can no longer be applied to what's in front of him.

The facts of the matter are these: Israfel is in love with Nate. Nate's interest in Israfel was sufficient for him to pursue his priest until Israfel, weak, succumbed. Israfel had thought that he was no more than a shameful notch on Nate's bedpost, until Nate yelled so many confusing things at him on the evening of Michael's visit, things about a *them* and *this* and *us* that Israfel hadn't dared to believe in. And now, apparently, Nate is avoiding not only Israfel, but his parents, too. Nate is sick, or pretending to be, and all of it is because of Israfel.

He doesn't know what to do. He has asked, and asked, and nobody has shown him what to do. Israfel sleeps fitfully, uncomfortably, plagued by his concerns. The obvious deduction, he is forced to concede, is that Nate is in love with him. It seems ludicrous, but given the facts, it seems horribly close to being the only possible conclusion. But then, what can that change? Even if they love each other, a relationship between them would still be wrong, in violation of the Church's position on the whole question of homosexuality.

And yet, if they do love each other....

He thinks, as if to try out the thought for size: *It isn't really love. It's only an imitation of love, sent by the Devil to push us into sin.*

His heart turns over uncomfortably, and he dismisses the thought immediately as a ridiculous falsehood. He loves Nate, and the fact that Nate is a boy doesn't render Israfel somehow incapable of processing his own feelings. They love each other.

He thinks about the old priest, and the resignation, the exhaustion in his voice. *I do not forget, my son.* He thinks about

Jesus, and the new covenant ratified through His blood. His Bible is sitting on the nightstand, in its usual place, and Israfel picks it up idly in one hand, turns the flimsy pages with the other until he finds the part he is interested in.

"For this is the covenant that I will make with the house of Israel after those days," declares the Lord: "I will put my laws into their minds, and write them on their hearts, and I will be their God, and they shall be my people. And they shall not teach, each one his neighbor and each one his brother, saying, 'Know the Lord,' for they shall all know me, from the least of them to the greatest. For I will be merciful toward their iniquities, and I will remember their sins no more." In speaking of a new covenant, He makes the first one obsolete. And what is becoming obsolete and growing old is ready to vanish away.

He thinks of Peter's vision of the clean and unclean, of his interpretation of it to the Gentile Cornelius: "Ye know how that it is an unlawful thing for a man that is a Jew to keep company, or come unto one of another nation; but God hath showed me that I should not call any man common or unclean."

It's confusing, he thinks. Everything is so *fucking* confusing. What is the dogma but a series of decisions made by centuries of priests, their own interpretations of a complicated text that contradicts itself at every turn? Paul is clear enough, but Israfel has never been much of an idolater of saints, unlike many a priest he has known, and Jesus was unhelpfully silent on the subject of people of Israfel's "temperament and inclination." The word of the Church is the word of men only, and Israfel wants the word of God.

"Please," he prays, aloud into the silence. "*Please*, Father, show me what to do!"

He would, at this stage, take anything as indication—a flicker of the lights, a rush of wind, a *sign*—but there is nothing. The silence continues silent. Israfel, for safety's sake, even attempts the old "open the Bible to an illuminating passage revealed to you by the hand of a benevolent God," his fingers trembling with anticipation.

He gets a passage about mold. It's not terribly enlightening, and Israfel swiftly closes the book again.

Perhaps tomorrow, he tells himself, as he shuts off the lights and gets into bed. Perhaps everything will be clear tomorrow.

Seventeen

HE'S standing in a field. Beyond this, Israfel is entirely at a loss as to where he is, but about the field part he's pretty certain. It's not a playing field, he doesn't think—not the kind of field where the village kids might go to kick a football around—but rather the kind of field that bears crops in the autumn and is fallowed and turned and made use of. A productive field, then. The mud clings thickly to Israfel's shoes.

He looks around uncertainly, looking for an explanation, or someone who might yield answers, but there is nothing. The field seems to go on endlessly, its dark ridges undulating to the horizon.

"Patience," says a voice, and it's nowhere and everywhere, at the back of his skull and behind his eyes, vibrating in every molecule of the air. He classifies it as a voice only because he knows no other word for it. It isn't something heard, nor even something received as words in his mind. He *feels* the instruction, and it takes on the form of words for him because he is too insignificant to understand it the way that it truly is.

For some reason, he feels exceptionally insignificant, just at this moment.

"I'm *being* patient," he tells the presence, whatever it might be. "I've *been* patient. This isn't easy for me, you know. I want some help."

He knows, somehow, that the presence has answers for him, if only he can drag them out of it. The presence is a soft hum around him, an electricity in the air. Israfel lifts his face, straining to be closer to it, to pin it down.

The presence is more than a little annoyed by this, Israfel senses. The "patience" note throbs again, more forcefully, in warning. Then, "Aren't things clear enough?"

The question wraps around him, sharp with the implication of annoyance. Israfel snorts. He's annoyed, too, abruptly, because *nothing* is clear. He's out here, alone, in a nowhere field, and some formless *thing* is telling him that everything should make sense.

"They really aren't," Israfel says, crossing his hands over his chest.

The presence huffs. For something with no body, no voice, no real physicality at all, it manages to convey a huff with surprising clarity. "You're just not listening," it says, accusation prickling up Israfel's spine like sparks, crackling in the air.

Israfel sighs. Exasperation, when the presence feels it like this, is not something it finds pleasant, and evidently protest is not the way to get on in this business. Whatever it is, the presence is big, bigger than anything he could imagine—so big that it has to come to him like this, in a place where even metaphor fails. Israfel doesn't want to offend it.

"Please," he says, gently. "*Please*. I'm trying, but I'm not... I'm obviously too stupid to read between the lines. I would really appreciate it"—and suddenly he's on his knees in the dirt, mud seeping damply through his trousers—"if you could tell me in small words what I need to do."

Nothing. For a moment, Israfel thinks perhaps he didn't make himself clear enough, that the presence doesn't know how to respond. But the gentle throb in the air seems to have disappeared entirely, and then Israfel is worried for entirely different reasons. He doesn't care to think what a thing like this could do if mortally upset. Perhaps it's gone away in search of backup.

The sudden light that splits the sky doesn't exactly assuage his concerns. It's bright, brighter than anything he's ever looked at directly in his life, brighter than the burn of the sun against his retinas on hot summer days. It peels up slowly from the horizon, spreading over the blue, until eventually everything is white, washed clean. It's shockingly, blindingly pure, brittle white fire, and Israfel knows that it should be too painful to look at it. But the light just continues to grow, flooding the field and licking over Israfel's skin, and somehow there's no ache, no pain in his eyes at all.

"Look," says the light, says the voice, and it's everywhere; it's inside him. "Look, Israfel, I think you expect too much. A sign doesn't need to be a letter appearing out of thin air, with God's signature scrawled across the bottom, you know."

Israfel bites his lip on a rueful smile. "I know that," he says. "I know, I just…."

"You just." The light pulses around him, irritated again. "I have a thousand and one things to do, and you just want a St. Peter Special, huh?" Another little pulse. "We were only supposed to have to do that once. You're meant to understand that it stands as a reference for other situations, but obviously that's too much for you people to grasp."

Israfel furrows his brow, raising his eyes to the light in appeal. He's not sure where exactly one is supposed to look when addressing an all-consuming, omnipresent form of energy, but he thinks he may as well make the attempt to be polite. "It's so hard to know," he says, pleadingly. "I just… I mean, the dogma says—"

"Do you worship the dogma, then?" the light pulses back at him. If it had been anything other than a mystic, prophetic light, Israfel might have said it sounded pissed off. "Or the Pope? Are we worshipping the Pope now? What did Father Francis say to you?"

Israfel remembers the old priest, the little old church. *I do not forget, my son.* "Well—"

"And what about the fourteen dreams, by my reckoning, I've already sent you?" The light flickers in something that might have been a scowl, if it had anything resembling a face. "You have your Bible, don't you? If we'd known how much trouble would come of that thing...."

Israfel laughs softly. He can't help it. "It's not exactly clear," he points out, and then colors a little. "Um. Sir."

A ripple, flooding him with a spike of something like amusement. "Do you know who I am?"

Israfel shakes his head. "My... psyche?"

"The clever ones think too much," says the light. It feels disgruntled. "I'm not your pitiful human psyche. I'm your namesake." The sky, without warning, suddenly breaks in two, darkness splitting the light, reforms in a flash, luminescent. "I'm an angel of the Lord. This gives me some authority."

Israfel blinks in startlement. "My... angel?"

"An angel," the light corrects him. I serve God. I do not serve man. I certainly do not serve you. I'm only here now because God is shocked by your inability to interpret a perfectly obvious chain of events. Stop trying to screw up your fate, Israfel."

"My fate?" Israfel screws up his face in consternation. "But... I don't...."

"Nate," the light blares at him, "natenatenate..." and it's everywhere, in his ears and his mind and his body, sudden sensation of Nate's presence and hands. When he opens his eyes, Nate is there, for a moment, in front of him, head cocked, smiling. Israfel has half reached out toward him before the light stops him, shimmering over the vision, blotting it from view.

"Nate," the vision repeats, firmly. "In a word," it reminds him, and its voice now sounds strangely more like it is beginning as words, rather than simply becoming them as it reaches Israfel's mind, "there are three things that last forever: faith, hope and love; but the greatest of them all is love".

Israfel is wide-eyed, his head full of too much blinding light. "The... Israfel...."

"Get a clue," spits the light, a riptide of irritation rising up Israfel's throat, exiting his mouth in waves. "You don't always have to listen to your brother. Try listening to your Father, sometimes."

The next thing he knows, Israfel is on his side in bed, temples pulsing with a furious headache, and his eyes burn as if he's been staring at the sun.

Israfel picks through the dream carefully, cautiously, like a man making his way through a morass. It could, he reasons, have been nothing more than a dream, a jumble of the day's thoughts poured into the tumbler of his mind and shaken to give him what he wanted to hear. But his eyes seem to ache a little more when he considers this possibility, as if with some residue of that angry light. Israfel is a man of faith, not a skeptic, and he can't forget what he was told. If the dream means what he thinks it means, then it is contrary, absolutely contrary, to the dogma of the Church, to the beliefs of the Papal See. But then, as the light said, he is supposed to worship God, not the Pope. If the Pope can dream that Mary was assumed bodily into Heaven, and then adapt the dogma to reflect this revelation, then surely Israfel can dream that love is love and have it be equally true? Even if there were no angels involved, not really, the dream might still mean *something*.

His chest prickles guiltily at the thought, for even daring to think it. But then he remembers the old priest and thinks... perhaps it isn't so ridiculous an idea. Jesus, after all, most certainly did not condemn homosexuality. Israfel has read many treatises suggesting that the sin of Sodom was not actually what is now called "sodomy," but licentiousness, hedonism, rape. Nobody is suggesting that a righteous man can be a rapist or a lech, a man who indulges his sexual appetites at the expense of others' happiness and dignity and sense of self-worth. But if a righteous man *can* fall in love with another man—as even the Catholic Church allows—then perhaps expression of that love does not equate to the sins of Sodom?

Israfel dares to test this idea in his mind, and the light seems to latch onto it, to illuminate it from the inside. These are no longer the days of Leviticus, of the Old Covenant, of sinful shellfish and evil mold. Nor are they, even, the days of St. Paul, when homosexual orgies were the common practice of many unchristian religions, and Paul's cautions were as much an attempt to distance his people from them as to distance them from their own feelings. Paul also suggests that Christian men must grow beards or be sinners, and Israfel doesn't exactly see a lot of people insisting upon *that*.

He sighs and slings his feet out of the bed.

He wants, suddenly and viscerally, to go to Nate. The more he thinks about it, the surer he feels that with Nate is where he needs to be: with him entirely, the way he was in all the dreams that his namesake, apparently, sent him. There was something about Nate that was different, Israfel knew from the beginning. He is not, has never been, undisciplined enough to simply fall for any pretty boy who crossed his path more than once. There was something about Nate, and Israfel can't dismiss the possibility that maybe, just maybe, he *is* fated for Israfel—that something about him makes him Israfel's intended.

It sounds stupid, put like that; ridiculous, and Israfel has to laugh a little, but the feeling doesn't go away. It's new, certainly, and he is still less than entirely convinced by it, but it's a stronger certainty than he's felt about any of this in weeks, and that isn't something he's willing to discard on a whim. Especially after everything his dream seemed to say.

He would have to leave the Church. The words feel strange in his mind. They ring hollow, unreal. He has been a member of the Church, tied to the priesthood, for eleven years now, and the idea of not having that is something that he can't quite wrap his mind around.

"I'd have to leave the Church," he announces to the quiet of his bedroom. There's more of a resonance, this way. The words begin to make sense, begin to *mean* something as they double back into his mind, as he hears them said. And they're... odd. The thought is odd, out of keeping with his idea of himself, with who he thinks he is. But then, what *is* Israfel, right now, but a hypocritical priest, unsuited for a vocation that was never really a vocation at all. He's used to this, and he's good at many aspects of it, but when he thinks about it, it's never come easily to him.

He's always had "the thing" inside of him, and it's always made him unhappy, even before Nate arrived and turned everything inside out. And now that there's a suggestion that he *could* have Nate, if only he were willing to give up the priesthood, the idea of the Church seems to yawn before him like an endless unhappiness, years of dark loneliness. It's not something a priest should ever feel about the prospect of ministry, and he knows it. It's not fair to a congregation, any more than it would be fair to himself, to go on in a path that holds no joy or luster for him, quite aside from the question of Nate.

He'll have to leave the Church. That much, though the prospect still seems unreal, is clear, and the more he rolls the thought about his head, the more obvious, the more necessary it seems.

It isn't, after all, as if there's nothing else he could do. Training for the priesthood is vigorous, deep, and expansive. Israfel would be well qualified to teach any number of subjects, either in a high school or at college level. He could be a classicist or a theologian, even a literature teacher. When he was in high school himself—he remembers, for the first time in years—he'd harbored a secret fetish for Latin, from the culture to the conjugations.

The trouble is that Nate is *seventeen*. He isn't old enough, Israfel thinks, to want someone like Israfel to show up on his doorstep and whisk him away into the night. Haul him off to some ill-defined new life removed from everything he's ever known. He still lives with his parents, for goodness' sake. Israfel can hardly expect him to leap at the idea of absconding with a twenty-nine year old failed priest, particularly after the earful he gave Israfel a few weeks previously. Equally evident, though, is the fact that Israfel can hardly embark upon this alone, without telling Nate of his intentions. Nate may be young, but he's older than his years, and Israfel, more than anybody, knows that he knows what he wants. It would be just as unfair of Israfel to quit his vocation *without* telling Nate that he's the motivating factor, as to try and foist upon him an adult relationship that he may or may not want.

The permutations of the thing are beyond Israfel's ability to untangle alone. The point is that Nate, on whatever level, is involved. No matter what Nate may feel—no matter how temporary a thing this may be for him—it isn't temporary for Israfel, and Nate has been responsible for making him, finally, recognize that. He deserves, at least, the opportunity to tell Israfel where he stands.

Whatever else he may decide to do, Israfel needs to talk to Nate first.

Eighteen

ISRAFEL can't remember the last time he genuinely debated what he ought to wear. One of the safest, most reassuring things about the priesthood is the uniform it's provided him for years, his armor against the world. He gets up. He puts on his cassock. He goes about his business. For services, he puts on his alb and cincture, another layer of protection. But Nate managed to do what nobody else has ever even attempted: pierced the armor effortlessly and reached the man underneath. Something tells Israfel that Nate should be repaid for his perceptiveness, that Israfel should greet him as he truly is, as Nate has made him see that he should be.

It isn't an easy decision to make. For one, Israfel isn't exactly sure how to begin orchestrating a visit to Nate, whose home he has never ventured near. He doubts that Captain and Mrs. Mulligan will be terribly pleased to have him invade their privacy on a hunt for their eldest son. He doubts even more that they'd be pleased to see him without his vestments. But Tom was very clear about the fact that Nate wasn't exactly venturing outside, and that leaves Israfel with limited options.

For an hour he frets about it, and then for another. By the time he's made his decision—fumbled into the pair of jeans he keeps in the back of his wardrobe for decorating, and similar dirty tasks—it's early afternoon. The jeans are ten years old and too tight around the hips and backside, but a T-shirt covers the worst of the evidence, keeps it from qualifying as obscene. He wants his sincerity to be obvious, wants Nate to believe him when he speaks, and this— Israfel outside in the street clothes of his teenage self—is the best he can come up with. He has a car and a cell phone with Nate's number in it. These will be his first weapons. But if they fail... well, Israfel will have a secondary line of attack.

When he reaches the house, it's quiet, the dim windows showing no signs of activity within. Israfel fidgets in his seat, instinct making him tug at the cap sleeves of his T-shirt, the waistband of his jeans. He feels strange, now, outside in public like this, as strange as if he were walking the streets in pajamas. A priest is expected to wear his cassock at all times when he might be seen by others, without exception.

But Israfel's decision is made: this will be his last day as a priest.

He hesitates for a long, long moment with his finger on the call button. It's dark inside, he reasons. Nate may not even be there. But Tom had been very clear about Nate's reluctance to leave his room, and Israfel knows that his excuses are only forms of procrastination. He steels himself. Eventually, sets his thumb on the button and presses.

It rings off. He's not terribly surprised.

He dials again, letting it ring out into nothingness. After a moment's pause, he tries again. And again. And again.

On the fifth try, Nate picks up, and Israfel almost drops the phone at the sound of his voice, his disgruntled, wary, "Hello?"

"Nate!" he says, voice strangely sharp with something misplaced, like surprise. He says Nate's name the way he might have shouted it if Nate were walking out into traffic, and the inappropriate tone gives Nate pause, makes him say, "Raf? You okay?"

"I'm outside," Israfel says. Evasion has never been his strong point. "I'm-I'm not okay. I mean. I guess I *am* okay, now, maybe, or I *could* be. But, Nate, I need to talk to you."

Nate gives him a second and then laughs, bemused and skeptical. "Raf, I haven't seen you in weeks, and apparently I'm the root of all evil. What the fuck do you think I could possibly want to talk to you about?"

Israfel doesn't hesitate. "I miss you," he says, his tone plaintive. "Nate, I-I need to tell you something, please. I don't really want to explain on the phone."

Nate snorts, harsh and cynical. "If this is gonna be all about how you want to start shit up again, then you've got another think coming, Padre. You can't throw me out like trash one second and try to drag me back for the sex the next."

The words are like a knife to the gut, and Israfel grits his teeth through the pain. "Nate," he says, trying desperately for rationality. "Nate, it's not like that. You haven't let me speak."

"And what would be the point, huh?" Nate's louder now, irritated. "You know it'd just be the same old fucking story. Scared little Father Israfel—it's fine for him to screw the altar boy as long as nobody *tells*. As long as word of his *sin* doesn't get out, you know. Why the fuck should I think anything would be different this time, Raf? Why the hell would I want to go back to you?"

"I'm leaving the priesthood," Israfel says, more abruptly than he intended. He knows it's too abrupt the moment it's out because Nate says nothing, only sits silently on the other end of the phone. Israfel takes a shaky breath. "I-I understand if you don't want anything more to do with me, Nate, I do. It's just that… you were right. I wanted to tell you that you were right, and I realize it now. I'm a hypocrite, living like this. I'm a hypocrite, and I'm a… I'm *gay*, like you said, so, yeah. I'm going across state later to tell the

Bishop." He pauses. "And I don't... I'm not asking anything from you, nothing like that. I just thought you should know."

The silence that follows is tortuous, tearing at his heart. When at last he hears Nate take a breath, he feels his own lungs working and realizes belatedly that he had been waiting to draw in air.

"You're... Raf, you're kidding me, right?"

Israfel laughs, a little harshly. "Not kidding." He pauses, chews on his lip a little. "Nate, where are you?"

"I'm in my room," Nate tells him, in a voice that is wary and slow. But the next moment, there's a yellow glow in the window of one of the street-facing upstairs rooms, and then Nate is there, the shape of him outlined behind the glass. "Is that you, lurking like a creeper in your car, huh?"

Israfel laughs again, and this time it's softer, relieved, the sound of tension collapsing at the warmth in Nate's voice, the familiarity of being insulted by him in the way that only Nate can turn insults into endearments. "Right here," he confirms, the corners of his mouth tugging upward against his will. "Come down here? I'd really rather explain this to your face."

"You just want to look at me," Nate says. The light clicks off.

"Maybe," Israfel teases, and the playfulness surges out of him like liberation. "But I can't, can I, if you're going to stay up there?"

Nate is at the front door in three seconds, out of it in another. Israfel debates whether or not to get out of the car to greet him, but he's too slow and Nate is too quick, throwing open the passenger door before he can so much as unfasten his seat belt.

"Whoa," Nate says, standing there with one hand still poised on the door. "You're not... Christ, Raf."

Israfel smiles a little sheepishly, spreading his hands. "Told you."

"Fuck," says Nate. He takes a breath, climbs into the seat, and slams the door behind him. "Fuck, Raf, where'd you even *get* those?" He reaches out, running his fingertips lightly up the denim over Israfel's thigh, and Israfel shivers involuntarily.

"Hey," he chides, turning the key in the ignition, "I was young once."

"Yeah, and now you're Methuselah," Nate snorts, rolling his eyes. He gestures toward the steering wheel, where Israfel's hands are now positioned and waiting. "What're you doing? You planning to kidnap me, or something?"

He's teasing, but Israfel's smile twitches a little nervously all the same. He removes his hands from the wheel, folding them in his lap. "No. I just thought we might be better off having this conversation in my house than in the street, that's all."

"Hey," Nate says, and the sudden mellowing of his tone tells Israfel that his own discomfort hasn't gone unnoticed. It never does, with Nate. He reads people far too well. Israfel can't believe he ever thought him unfeeling. Nate reaches out, thumbs the line of Israfel's jaw, and Israfel turns his face into the touch unconsciously.

"Hey," Nate says. "I was kidding. Nothing about us is like that, okay? You're not making me do anything. You never have. And I don't feel *obligated* because you've finally come to your senses, okay, before you run off down that road."

Israfel opens his mouth to protest, and then closes it again, stumped. Nate smiles. And then, with absolute, unpracticed ease, he leans across the gearstick and presses his mouth to Israfel's, like it's nothing and everything. It's not even a kiss, at first, just a soft touch of lips, but then Israfel makes a soft little sound into it, and Nate's mouth opens, a damp, gentle heat against Israfel's.

It's December, and dusky with it, but it's not dark, not yet. Anyone could walk by and see them like this, Israfel's fingers creeping up into Nate's hair, Nate's hands cradling Israfel's jaw as he licks his mouth open. The flickers of Israfel's anxious instincts are still there, but he suppresses them with an ease that surprises him, leaning into the kiss instead.

It doesn't matter, he realizes, the thought suddenly blindingly clear in his mind. It doesn't matter who sees them, not any more.

The age of consent in this state is seventeen, and Israfel has defrocked himself, and in this moment, he feels untouchable.

It's not, of course, *entirely* true. Israfel has yet to inform the Bishop of his decision, and he certainly—the mere thought sends shivers up his spine—would not like Nate's parents to find them out like this. Truthfully, he wouldn't like them to find out at all, but they'll cross that bridge when they come to it, and he knows that it may have to be crossed. For now, "not like this" will do. Gently, and not a little reluctantly, he pulls away from Nate.

"Come home with me," he says, thumb smoothing over the sharp line of Nate's cheekbone. "It's not that... I just—"

Nate forestalls his explanations with a grin, sits back in his own seat and straps in. "It's okay," he says. "I'd really prefer to do this in your bed too."

Ordinarily, Israfel is an extremely careful driver. But with Nate in the passenger seat, palm resting lightly on Israfel's thigh, the village's thirty miles an hour speed limit seems suddenly ridiculously slow. He nudges up to thirty-five, forcing himself not to kick it higher, and Nate laughs at his difficulty, palm riding up a little, its teasing pressure a promise.

It's not as if it's only for sex that Israfel is doing this. Hell, it's not even the sex that motivates him most, so much as it is the feeling that everyone deserves companionship and the knowledge that he wants a *male* companion, wants *Nate*. Probably, they should talk about this properly, reason and discuss. The fact of the matter is that Nate may not want what Israfel wishes he would, and though the thought makes him cold, he knows he needs to ask the question.

Right now, though, there isn't time for any of that. Israfel is riding an adrenaline high, and Nate's fingers are riding the cut of his hipbone. Nate may be the only teenager in the car, but fuck it, Israfel is young, too. He feels younger with Nate than he can ever remember feeling when he was seventeen himself. Nate makes him want to do wild things, gets inside of him like a pathogen in the blood, and Israfel *wants* it. If this is a disease, Israfel wants to surrender to every one of its symptoms.

They reach the rectory in record time. Nate's fingers are slipping beneath the waistband of Israfel's jeans before he's even done locking the door behind them, and the frantic pace, the frenzy to it is like the first time, the two of them shedding clothes in the doorway in their haste. In every other aspect, though, it's as if they're living in a different world. Israfel's hands transmit all his love and want as they smooth over Nate's skin, without the tarnished taste of guilt in the back of his throat. Nate is warm against him, perfect, the knobs of his spine drawing Israfel's fingers downward.

Somehow, Israfel gets them up the stairs. Nate, he's sure, would have been happy to make use of the guest room, or even, at a push, the sofa, but that isn't what Israfel wants. If they're going to do this, for the first time, without the dark twist of unhappiness in Israfel's stomach, then everything about it must be above board, must be real. There's nothing secretive to the loose fall of Nate's limbs on Israfel's bed, nor the way he lifts his hips to let himself be divested of his underwear. Israfel breathes deep at the sight of him, all angles and curves, Michelangelo's David. He cannot help but think, if only for a moment, of the real David, and the man who loved him. Jonathan, shedding his armor, standing vulnerable before a boy he barely knew and yet loved already. Israfel has always been vulnerable before Nate, but only now does he really see that Nate would never, *could* never have hurt him.

Naked, Nate's body is living evidence of the fineness of God's work, the multifaceted glory of His perfect creation. Seeing him like this, Israfel feels he can understand why the ancients so idolized young men. There is something undeniably compelling about their unblemished strength, new muscle seen in tandem with subtle touches of femininity. No blind chance, Israfel thinks, could have carved a mouth like Nate's, nor anything as perfect as the shadowed place where his pelvis meets his abdomen. He is no divinity, but he is all the proof Israfel needs that the divine exists, transmuting dust into works of living art.

Israfel cradles Nate's heel in his palm, turns the foot gently outward. At the touch of Israfel's half-open mouth to the knob of his anklebone, Nate draws in a breath, foot jerking in surprise.

"Shh," Israfel soothes, trails his mouth slowly up the inside of Nate's calf. Nate is breathing hard underneath him, fingers tangling in Israfel's hair. His tugging suggests impatience, but Israfel is in no mood to hurry—not with so much beauty to be mapped, for once, with no sour taste of contrition under his tongue. Nate's legs tremble, fall open, as Israfel moves, tongue tracing a fine line of heat up the fine skin of Nate's inner thigh. Nate's gasping, now, hips twitching upward in expectation, and Israfel smiles, smoothing his thumbs over Nate's hipbones. The muscles in Nate's stomach twitch at the proximity.

"Turn over," Israfel says, voice barely more than a whisper.

The sound Nate makes at that is like nothing on earth. He closes his eyes, reaches out to rub the heel of his hand up the spine of Israfel's cock, hard and leaking slick against his belly. Israfel hisses through his teeth, catches Nate's hand and pins it, thumb stroking idly over the first two knuckles.

"Nate," he insists, low and soft with heat. Nate swallows visibly and rolls over, obedient, onto his stomach.

Nate's back is an undiscovered country, its lines and valleys new territory for Israfel's hands. Nate is shivering finely, tensed, waiting for something, but Israfel is not in any sort of hurry. He shifts on the bed, pulls himself upward to straddle Nate's hips, and mouths at the uppermost vertebra of his spine. At Nate's soft whimper, he bites there, laves the marks with his tongue, and bites again. Nate squirms underneath him, the motion smearing Israfel's slick between them at the small of Nate's back. Israfel hums in his throat, slides a hand up the back of Nate's neck and into his hair, tugging his head forward. The gesture bares Nate's nape to Israfel's mouth, and he teethes at it, drawing the blood to the surface, making a mark.

The sounds Nate makes when he's touched have always sparked a heat in Israfel, and the sounds he makes now are no exception. Israfel stifles a groan against the back of Nate's neck, wriggles a little lower, biting at the wings of his shoulder blades and then retracing the paths with his tongue. Nate is like a mad thing beneath him, bucking and moaning, his body twisting violently at every touch of Israfel's mouth. His backside is jutting up into the shallow pan of Israfel's pelvis, every twist and turn of Nate's body thundering back against Israfel's cock. It's too much, like this, too good, and Israfel makes himself slip lower, nipping a line of heat down the knobs of Nate's spine. When he reaches the base of it, his hands are firm on Nate's waist, holding him still against the onslaught of tongue.

For a long moment, Nate seems curiously compliant, holding his breath as Israfel sucks a bruise into his lower back. But then Israfel moves, slides his mouth wetly up Nate's spine again, and Nate lets out a low groan of frustration, hand coming up behind himself to find Israfel's hair and pull.

"Raf, for cryin' out loud," he rasps, in a voice that sounds overused and raw. "Please, dammit, I *get* it, but could you please just fuck me?"

Israfel pauses in the action of stroking up over Nate's shoulder blade, thumb poised at the lower point of it. It isn't as if what Nate is suggesting has never crossed his mind. Of course, during his more reckless nocturnal contemplations, it has. But he's never let himself be so deluded as to think Nate might *want* that, Israfel splitting him apart, burning himself into him. He hitches a breath, rubs his mouth against Nate's shoulder blade, fumbling for words.

"You don't...," he manages. "Nate, I don't... you don't have to. I mean, I don't *expect*—"

There's something like a sigh, and then Nate is rolling gracefully onto his back beneath him, lifting his knees so that Israfel is cradled between. "*I* expect," Nate tells him harshly, and then laughs. "*Stupid*. Raf, come on. I want it." He lifts his hips, and the brush of their cocks makes Israfel bite his lip on a moan. Nate smiles, the afternoon light glinting on his teeth.

"Want it," he says again. He rolls his hips and grinds himself up against Israfel. "Feels good. Wanted this with you for a while."

Israfel's mouth is dry, and he swallows, buying time. His pulse is thundering in his chest, in his groin, and he wants nothing more than to hitch Nate open and thrust deep into him, but still, "I just... Nate, I don't...."

"I'll show you," Nate says, reaching a long arm in the direction of the nightstand.

He's back in a moment with quantities of pink lotion in the palm of his hand. He laughs when he sees Israfel's expression and then bucks his hips again, as if to see a different one.

"It's not optimal," he explains, "but it'll do. I've done it before."

And then he's shifting upward, spreading his legs and slipping his fingers between them. Israfel feels as if he should look away, give him some privacy or something, but there's something transfixing about it: the way Nate's fingers find the place and circle; the way they slip slickly inside.

I'll be there, soon, Israfel thinks, and then flushes all over with it. "God," he breathes, half consciously, "Nate. That's so—" He bites his lip, words breaking up in his throat before he can urge them past his lips, but Nate doesn't seem to mind, angling his hips instead so that Israfel can see more clearly.

"You like that, huh?" He's sheened in sweat, the hollows of his throat and clavicle gleaming with the wet of it. His fingers press, smooth and slow, into himself, crook, and slide back out, and Israfel watches the clench of his body, the way it seems to *want*.

"There's this place inside," Nate explains, "and it feels like... *Christ!*" He throws his head back, hips arching up, pulse of pre-come slicking his belly. He's gorgeous like this, so fucking gorgeous, and Israfel can't keep back his strangled sound of approval, can't stay his hand. He lays a forefinger almost reverently at the place where Nate's knuckles meet the rim of him, where his fingers disappear, and Nate groans low and wanting, rolling his hips unselfconsciously.

"Push it in," Nate pants. "Fuck, *Raf*, go on, do it."

This time, Israfel doesn't hesitate. It's what he wants, after all. What his body wants to do, and he lets himself sink into the instinct. Nate takes him beautifully, envelops him as if he were made for this, his body splaying wider to accommodate the new intrusion. He's tight inside, ridiculously so, and Israfel moans even as Nate does, at the slide of their fingers together, the clench of muscle around them.

"Now," Nate grits out, lifting his free hand to press the palm to Israfel's heart. "Now, Raf, *please*."

They withdraw their fingers together, and Nate interlaces their hands for a moment afterward, heedless of the stickiness of body-warm lotion clinging to their skin. "You've never done this?" Nate's hand shifts, curling around the base of Israfel's cock, eyes locked on his.

Israfel shakes his head tightly, not daring to breathe, but Nate doesn't seem to require any more of an answer. He lifts his hips, tugs, and then all at once Israfel is there, bluntly pressing inside, Nate's heartbeat pulsing tightly around the head of him. It's good, fuck, *incredible* to think that he's thrusting into Nate, that Nate would take him willingly, even eagerly into his body. Nate lifts his legs, hooking them around Israfel's waist, and nudges with his heels, and the slow slide forward is like an ascent into joy.

Nate is pure heat underneath him, around him, everywhere, and Israfel feels the metronome of Nate's pulse overriding his own. He jerks his hips, involuntary, and Nate cries out, tugs at his hair and arches, wanting closer, *more*. Israfel is more than happy to oblige.

It's clumsy, at first. Everything's harder than it looks, the friction of Nate's body unbelievable around him and the bucking of their hips taking a moment to fall into rhythm. It doesn't matter, though. Nothing matters but the closeness of Nate, the way they interlock like cogs, turning together. Israfel is breathless with it, almost tearful with the thought that he could have lost this, would have willingly rejected this intimacy, this most holy and transcendent joining. Nate is scrabbling at his back, licking at his jaw, and Israfel rubs their mouths together blindly, letting Nate urge him with a foot at the small of his back.

"Nate," he breathes, "*Nate….*" and Nate hums as if in agreement, rolling his hips to meet Israfel's thrusts, the motions of his pelvis. Israfel's arms are beginning to burn, the muscles twitching all the way to the shoulder with effort, but Nate is moving faster, now. He twists his hips on a thrust back and cries out, and Israfel couldn't stop if his life depended on it, never mind his arms.

"*There,*" Nate's gasping, clawing at Israfel's hair, at his shoulders, "Fuck, *there* ohJesuslike*that*…." And Israfel's lost his anchor to reality somewhere along the way, is seeing stars and colors and a brightness that is all Nate. He's making little sounds, he can tell, can feel them in his throat, but Nate is half keening, so it hardly signifies.

"Nate," he's panting, in between nips at Nate's mouth, licks at his throat, "God, Nate, you know I love you," and Nate snaps up in an impossible arc and comes with a cry like dying, like seeing another world.

The clench of his body in its climax is more than Israfel can take. His thrusts are erratic, now, stuttering into Nate's convulsive heat, and the light is building up behind his eyes, indefatigable. Israfel has no wish to hold out on it, not when Nate is waiting already somewhere in that brightness.

Nate is still moving with him as Israfel spends himself inside him, still petting his hair with weak, shivery hands. He cries out something, pulses and pulses, releasing himself, and Nate is there, steadfast, to catch him. Afterward, he lays his damp face on Nate's damp shoulder, tangling their legs as he struggles for air.

Left to his own devices, Israfel would happily have lain there until he fell asleep, sated and stunned. But Nate shifts, after a long moment, laughing a little as he shoves at Israfel's hips.

"Raf," he murmurs, hooks his foot around Israfel's calf. "I, um." He gestures vaguely at their bodies, still joined.

It takes Israfel a second to discern his meaning. The moment he does, his face floods immediately with heat, and he covers his smile of embarrassment with his shoulder. "Oh. *Oh.* God, Nate, I'm sorry, I didn't...."

But Nate's laughing, looking fondly on his agitation. "S'okay, I'll live. Truth be told, I don't really want you to go anywhere, either." His eyes go soft for a moment, and Israfel feels something grow three sizes, somewhere in the region of his heart. Nate shakes his head, smiling. "But if you don't pull out, I'll probably clamp back down on you, and that might be kinda painful, so...."

"Of course," Israfel assures him hastily, pulling himself up on his elbows. "Of course. Let me just...."

Nate guides the pace of it, slows his withdrawal with his hands. The dribble of ejaculate that emerges afterward bemuses him for a half second, before it occurs to him, far too belatedly, that something has been forgotten here.

"Oh," he says dubiously, trailing a finger through the whiteness on the inside of Nate's thigh. "Should we have... you know?" He mimes something, coloring, and thankfully Nate gets the picture.

"Aren't they bad?" he teases, tracing his thumb along Israfel's lower lip, corner to corner. Israfel laughs a little, ducks his head.

"So said a dream the Pope had, or something. Some total misinterpretation of the story of Onan. But it isn't as if you're any more likely to get pregnant without one, is it?"

Nate snorts a laugh and shakes his head. "Nah. And you're not going to get anything from me, either, if that's what you're worried about."

Israfel wrinkles his nose, curious despite his relief. "Have you been tested or something?"

Nate shakes his head, pulls himself up on his elbows and reaches for a tissue. "Never done that before, though. Or anything, actually, without a condom. And since you were a virgin, I think that puts us in the clear."

Israfel pauses mid-motion, eyes widening in surprise. "That was your first try? But I thought you said you'd done it before?"

"I didn't," Nate counters, returning with a fistful of Kleenex. "Said I'd opened myself up before, with lotion." He winks. "Thinking of you, of course."

Israfel laughs, but if he's truthful, he doesn't feel much like laughing. It's *beyond* laughter, this strange happiness welling up inside him, the sense of blessed privilege. He would have wanted Nate if Nate had been a former hustler, but knowing that nobody has ever felt what he has felt—that Nate has kept this, in whatever fashion, for him—the thought warms him in ways he cannot articulate.

"Nate," he ventures, slumping back down onto his side. "What I... what I said...."

"I figured," Nate tells him softly, depositing the Kleenex in a pile by the bed to be picked up later. He shifts down, too, fits his long body to Israfel's, shoulder to toe. "I didn't exactly think you'd be likely to throw in the whole priesthood towel, otherwise."

Israfel smiles, despite himself, at Nate's choice of words. The image of himself throwing a dishrag at the Bishop's feet is a welcome alternative to the way he has been picturing events up to now. "Well, no," he confesses, quietly. "But you don't... I mean, I need you to understand that I don't *expect*—"

"And again," Nate breaks in, "I do." He pauses for a moment, studying Israfel's face. Then, "*I do,*" he repeats earnestly, his eyes steady and sure. His tone says more than his words, and Israfel knows it, could not possibly fail to realize it.

He doesn't have words—doesn't even know what he'd say if he could. He pulls Nate forward, instead, and licks languidly into his mouth, letting everything he feels rush up out of him and into Nate. Nate hums against him, fingers curling at Israfel's waist. He doesn't say anything, but Israfel knows, somehow, that everything has been understood.

Some things about each other, they just know, he and Nate. It's always been that way. Israfel would love to think it could remain so.

Nineteen

THEY fall asleep, of course. It's the way they do things. It's late evening when they wake, the bedroom dark with shadows, Nate's body a solid warmth in Israfel's arms.

There are a lot of things to be discussed. Israfel would happily put them off for as long as possible, but Nate has cautioned him about that tendency before. From here on out, his life will be as clean a sheet as he can make it, and that means bringing up issues as they occur to him.

The first issue, obviously, is Nate.

He has to be cautious, the ground still muddy and uncertain. Nate loves him. That much, at least, Nate has made quite clear. But Israfel would have to be a fool to take for granted that a boy like Nate would want a man like him, wholly and entirely, on the basis of love alone. Nate's so *young*, he reasons. He won't want to be an outcast.

And then he remembers Nate's fervency, the outrage in his voice as he cited Israfel's many hypocrisies, called him on every truth he'd never let himself own up to. Nate is a man, and not one who'll be content to live a half life with people whose tolerance won't extend to his lifestyle choices. Israfel doesn't want to assume, but he doesn't want to offend, either. Not when there is so much foundation for hope.

They're dressed again before he manages to bring it up naturally, as Nate is combing through the kitchen cupboards for sustenance.

"You know I'll have to leave the rectory," he says, going for casual.

Nate pulls a face, but not one that harbors any surprise. Figures, Israfel thinks, that he's smart enough to have worked this out on his own. "How long'll they give you, do you think?"

Israfel shrugs. He's wondered this more than once himself, but, "Doesn't really matter," he says, shoving his hands into his trouser pockets. "I don't think I could really stand to stay here once I've dropped the anvil. The people here are nice, but they're terribly devout. I can't imagine they'd be very forgiving."

"I think you're right there," Nate tells him. The toast pops, and he catches it deftly, tosses it onto a plate before it can burn his fingers. "Any idea where you might go?"

And that, Israfel thinks wryly, is the ultimate question. He has no desire at all to return to Minnesota, a place he never harbored any great attachment to. Any of the things he's tentatively thought about doing could really be done anywhere, which makes decision making difficult. If he's considered anything, it's the possibility of finding some place close, so at least he'd be within striking distance of Nate.

"None at all," is what he says aloud. Mostly, it's true.

"Mind if I make a suggestion?"

Israfel blinks. He isn't sure what exactly he was expecting, but that certainly wasn't it. He studies Nate's face, but the expression there is nonchalant as he chews on a corner of his toast. Israfel shrugs, but the look he wears is inquisitive. "All suggestions welcome, I suppose. Go ahead."

Nate's still chewing, so Israfel has a moment to wait before he's swallowed and ready. "Well," he says, eventually, setting the plate back down on the countertop, "I was thinking. All the schools I've applied to are in California. And"—he clears his throat— "not to push it, but I think I have a good chance of being accepted by all of 'em."

Israfel frowns. It isn't really the expression he wants—doesn't convey any of the mixed-up things he's feeling, hearing those words come out of Nate's mouth—but it's the best he can manage for now, at least until he's got things straight. "Colleges? You're going to start college in California next summer?" He blinks. "I'm surprised your parents would let you go so far from home."

Nate shrugs elaborately, all loose limbs and bravado. "Eh. Well, I didn't tell them. But I got done with my SAT six months ago—1490, before you ask. Subject tests too, a few 700s in there. And I'll be eighteen on January 24. It's not like they can really stop me."

"Fourteen-ninety, huh?" Israfel laughs, can't seem to stop himself. "My goodness, Nate, I always knew you were smarter than you let on." He whistles softly, considering. "A lot of good schools would probably give you a full ride based on that."

"Provided they take homeschooled kids," Nate says, nodding like he's thought about this, as, evidently, he has. "Places I applied to all do, and anyway, Tommy and me've been standardized tested out the wazoo, make sure we're actually learning something."

"So you're saying," Israfel begins, his heart thrumming nervously in his chest, "You're saying... you think I should move out to California, because that's where you'll be by the time fall rolls around?"

Nate barks a laugh, rolling his eyes in exasperation. "*No*, Raf. Jeez, are you being deliberately dense, or something?" He crosses the little kitchen in a brief space of steps, reaching up to take Israfel's face between his hands. "What I'm *saying*, dope, is that I'm done with school. I'm gonna be eighteen in a few weeks, and it'd be useful to my non-negotiable future plans if I were in California already. And, you know, cutting my freaky-conservative parents loose was always gonna be great, but this way, all kinds of amazing things have converged at once." He tips his head, brushing his mouth against Israfel's. "I'm saying that, since what I really want is now actually available, I'd really love the chance to actually have it, please." He snorts. "Did you really think I was gonna just say goodbye to you, after all this? We're gonna go out to California *together*, dude. As soon as we can swing it. And then by the time school starts up, you'll be properly settled with a job, and we'll have an apartment, and everyone'll be jealous as fuck of the fact that I live with *you*."

Israfel registers that his face is hurting before he works out that the reason for the pain is a grin so broad that it seems to be trying to split his skull in two. It's on the tip of his tongue to say, just to be *sure*, "Do you mean it?" but the look on Nate's face says that such an inquiry would be not only unwelcome, but completely redundant. Nate means it, and Israfel feels that he could fly right now, if only someone would show him where to begin.

"So," Nate says, "Can I take that grin for a yes?"

The grin trips into a laugh, which trips into a series of kisses that map Nate's face from forehead to chin. "*Yes*, you may take it for a yes," Israfel assures him, firmly.

"Awesome," Nate says, and it's understated, but that's Nate all over. The green of his eyes burns gold and grey, lit up from the inside with his fervor. "So, when exactly were you planning on ditching the Bishop's skinny white ass?"

THE next few hours devolve into an unanticipated planning session, tight and exhaustive as any military briefing. By the time Nate has reluctantly agreed that he really should go home, the shape of things has started to emerge in outline, the details ironed out into something that they both hope will fly.

The next morning sees Israfel buttoning himself into his cassock, exactly as he has done most mornings for the past eleven years. It's a little anticlimactic, certainly, but the fact is that December is the busiest time in a priest's calendar, with the possible exception of Lent. While Israfel had been all in favor of throwing his vestments immediately at the Bishop's feet, Nate had pointed out that this would leave a lot of things in disarray, right when people would be expecting order and organization. Better, surely, to see things through the Christmas period and leave the announcements for the New Year. After all, it isn't exactly as if Israfel has stopped believing in God, Nate pointed out, very reasonably. It's just that he's now seen the light with regard to some of the other aspects of this particular organized religion and isn't too sure that God would like them much either. For the sake of a few Advent masses and a big Christmas Mass he could probably give in his sleep, Israfel is pretty much in agreement that cutting his losses for a while is the honorable thing to do.

Nate puts all his points in ways that revolve around the good of the parish, and certainly, the lack of a priest at Christmas would throw the whole village into disarray. But Israfel isn't stupid. The other angle at work here is quite obvious. He doesn't know the Mulligans terribly well, but he's seen enough of them to be fairly sure of what their reaction to any announcement from Nate will be. If Nate wants a last good Christmas with his parents—wants, moreover, not to ruin Christmas for Tommy, which is always a consideration for Nate—then Israfel will keep his office for a few more weeks to make that happen. It isn't as if it's a tortuous job, after all. Especially not now that Israfel has something else to look forward to.

Christmas in this parish is a mostly self-perpetuating exercise. Very little is required of Israfel in terms of organization, beyond his basic homilies and masses, because everything always happens in exactly the same way as it's happened since time immemorial. The bake sales and parish fetes are rolled out by the older ladies of the parish, as usual, and Israfel shows up when invited to be stuffed full of chocolate and pie. Nate, never one to miss an opportunity for pie, appears at all the same events and mostly behaves himself, although there are a couple of occasions when Israfel has to look away from his enthusiastic attentions to his fork. Good pie is good pie, but Nate knows exactly how to push his buttons, and Israfel isn't really willing to give him the benefit of the doubt about this.

About other things, of course, different rules apply. Israfel has acquired a lot of reading material since the time of his great revelation, and for the most part it has only served to bolster his convictions that this is the right thing to do. He loves Nate, ridiculously, devotedly, and all love comes from God. The Quakers, he notes with surprise, are accepting of gay marriage. There are any number of other denominations—particularly in the more liberal states, like California—that would support his contention that his love for Nate is not an affront to Christianity, but a validation of it, a manifestation of the greater, perpetual love of God. By and large, Israfel has done an admirable job of *not* doubting himself on this score.

Then there is the question of Nate: Nate's youth, Nate's parents. That Nate wants to come with him, Israfel is very well convinced. That this is an all-around good idea is something he feels the need to check with Nate from time to time, just so that everybody knows the score.

"You're *sure*," he says, picking nervously at the sleeve of his cassock. "You are *sure* you want to do this, Nate?"

Nate shrugs, kicking up his heel against the wall of the sacristy, hands shoved into his pockets. "Was gonna do it anyway, Raf. Hence the college applications. I couldn't've put up with their crazy for much longer." He snorts. "You think I want to stick around, listen to my father say 'those people should all be drowned at birth' whenever there's any mention of us?"

The "us" is pointed, emphatic, and even while the thought of Captain Mulligan saying such things is chilling, the defensiveness in Nate's voice warms Israfel a little. Nate is sure, and Israfel has always been grateful for this about him.

"But you could have gone to college," he pursues, "and not actually told them anything, you know. What are they going to say if you run away?"

Nate sighs, bites his lip, and looks down, and then glances up at Israfel under his eyelashes, his expression almost apologetic. "You're confusing me with you," he says wryly. "I tend to like openness, as a concept. I mean, hell, I know when to keep my mouth shut for my own good—like, oh, for the past five years or so." He laughs a little. "But I was gonna tell them anyway when I left, dude. The chances of me goin' away to college and ending up with some guy were pretty high, and I wasn't about to come home for break and lie about that. I'll tell them the score, and what they do with it is their bag." He shrugs. "I pretty much expect to be thrown out of the house, but that's not gonna matter when it comes to the point, is it? And, you know, I may be speaking out of turn here, but I doubt it'll be forever. Dad'll shout and scream and threaten, and Mom'll be upset and disappointed, but she wouldn't just... never talk to me again."

"And Tom?" Israfel prompts quietly.

Nate rubs at the back of his neck. "He knows the plan," he confesses. "All of it. I gave him my old cell phone so's we could call him when we get where we're going—tell him where we are without my parents listening in. It'll suck for him, but it's not like I'm leaving him in some pit of abuse or anything. They're bigots, but Tommy's too old and too smart now to fall for it. He's had enough education from me to know better."

Israfel smiles softly, one hand coming up to stroke over the point of Nate's shoulder. "How did *you* ever know better, Nate?" he asks curiously. It's something he's often wondered about, and he doesn't want to pass up the opportunity to ask.

"I read, don't I?" Nate shoots back. He shrugs again. "I know how I feel, man. Wasn't gonna waste my time crying about it when I could just go look up shit about it on the Internet in the library. Turned out that most people actually don't give a fuck about it, and that was enough for me."

It makes sense, really. Nate's incredibly self-sufficient and very mature for his years. Israfel would never have had the wherewithal or the confidence to do something like that. Although, to be fair, Israfel also would not have had recourse to the Internet. "You're braver than I am," he tells Nate, with a little shake of his head.

"Better not be," Nate retorts. "I only have to tell my Mom and Dad—and I probably won't tell them it's you I'm running off with, either, although I'm sure they might be capable of putting two and two together and not getting five, since you'll have vanished from view by then. You still have to tell the Bishop."

Israfel bites his lip on a smile that's half a grimace. "I know," he says wryly. "Believe me, Nate, I hadn't forgotten."

Twenty

HE GOES to see the Bishop on the morning after Epiphany, January 7. The irony isn't lost on him, but somehow he feels that the Bishop is rather less amused by it. It's a terse meeting, politely curt, their remarks to each other ringing strangely hollow in Israfel's ears. He isn't sure whether it makes it better or worse that he barely knows this man. Has met him, in fact, on only a couple of occasions, and never for very long. Israfel knew the bishop of his former diocese very well, and had done so since his early days in the seminary. He imagines that a meeting with him would have been rather less brittle. But then, it might have been harder to steel himself against fond disappointment than against blank disapproval of the sort the current bishop directs toward him. Probably, things are easier this way.

Procedurally, it's an oddly simple thing. Israfel says "yes" and "no" in all the right places. The Bishop makes no attempt at all to persuade him to stay, which, given his disclosures, Israfel hardly expected him to. He does implore Israfel to turn away from his sin, but it isn't as if Israfel wasn't anticipating something of the sort. The

Bishop gives him a week to clear out of the rectory, in a burst of generosity Israfel would not have predicted, but ultimately, Israfel feels as if he's waited long enough. The rectory came furnished when he arrived, and Israfel's possessions are few. Most of them have been packed up and waiting for weeks now.

He doesn't say goodbye to the congregation. This is, he supposes, something of a cowardly decision on his part, but he really doesn't know what he could possibly tell them. He has resigned his office. He is leaving the priesthood. These things will be made clear to them soon enough by an order from the Bishop. Beyond this, he has no wish to elaborate further. Undoubtedly a rumor will leak out at some point, but Israfel would like to be long gone before it does.

On January 8, Israfel leaves town. He takes with him his car and his laptop, his few clothes, and his truly incredible number of books. Everything else he's ever owned is still where he left it when he moved into the seminary, in the house he and Michael grew up in down in Minnesota. He hasn't given a great deal of thought to his parents since he came to this parish, hasn't seen them in some time. He is in no hurry, certainly, to make any declarations to them. In truth, though, he thinks, as he drives the empty road out of town, they have never been much for pushing their children, one way or the other. That was always Michael's role, and Israfel is beyond pandering to him. Michael will either overcome his anger, or Israfel will simply have no more to do with him. On this score, he is resigned. As for their parents, Israfel cannot help but think that this could hardly come as a surprise to them. They had never been as sold as Michael was on the idea of Israfel entering the priesthood, nor even upon the correction therapy Michael had led them all toward. Israfel can almost hear his father's comment: "Well, son, you tried." He isn't their favorite—never has been—but they're pragmatic people, undramatic and reasonable. They will never be entirely comfortable with the thought of him with Nate, but he is seventy-five percent sure that there'll be no disowning, either.

The remaining twenty-five percent isn't worth worrying about. Israfel's parents, after all, have played only a small part in his life for a decade, now. Nate, on the other hand, has taken upon himself a leading role, and Israfel has no intention of letting that be altered now.

Israfel lives in a motel in the next town for the following sixteen days. He and Nate communicate by text message, just staying in touch, but for the most part, there's nothing of importance left to arrange. It's a long two weeks, holed up alone in a nowhere town, but Israfel has a number of tasks that need to be taken care of. By the time Nate's birthday rolls around, Israfel has found them a small apartment in a not-too-murderous area of San Diego, deposit to be paid upon arrival. Also fully planned out are their journey directions, including stops along the way. The lease on the apartment is a short one, such that they'll be able to move without any great difficulty if they need to, but Israfel knows that UC San Diego will be Nate's first choice, if he receives more than one offer. Privately, Israfel fully expects him to be made several. But then, of course, Israfel is rather biased when it comes to Nate.

On January 24, Nate Mulligan turns eighteen. The following evening sees Israfel waiting, as planned, in the street outside the Mulligans' house, praying fervently that everything will have progressed smoothly. Things may have been arranged and rearranged to the very last detail, but still, Israfel can't help remembering Robbie Burns' "best laid schemes o' mice an' men." The last thing he wants is for things to "gang agley" now.

Nate comes out of the house at four minutes after seven. He was supposed to have been out by seven o'clock, but Israfel is forced to conclude that, as far as deviations go, this one is pretty minor. Israfel sees him in silhouette first, outlined against the rectangular glow of the open front door, suitcase in hand. It's so clearly Nate, and he's so obviously both alone and leaving that Israfel's anxious heart does a strange little leap in his chest, like it's shaking off the nerves of all the waiting. All those weeks imagining this in the In-n-Out Motel, and Israfel never realized until now that he wasn't sure it would happen—would never quite believe until he saw it: Nate, striding out across his parents' front lawn toward him.

For an ex-priest, Israfel has a surprising amount of trouble with faith. He likes to see things for himself before he believes them. But then, God's been helping him out a lot on that score lately. He sends up a little prayer of thanks as Nate lifts his free hand to wave at him, winds down the window and waves back.

They planned out this moment to the letter, all those weeks ago. Israfel is supposed to stay put in the car until Nate reaches him, foot poised over the pedal. After all, Israfel doesn't know yet what exactly has been said inside the house, and Nate doesn't want to chance anything when he might be in need of a clean getaway. But the look on Nate's face is more than a little reassuring, and Israfel has been in this car for a *very* long time. Nate's alone, and the suitcase in his hand looks heavy. He barely thinks twice before climbing out of the car to take it from him.

This, of course, is the moment that the front door swings open again. Israfel's frozen with one hand on the trunk of his car and the other clutching Nate's suitcase, in a position that might have been comical if he hadn't been in shock. He blinks up at the open door, wide-eyed and stock-still as a deer in headlights.

"Nate," comes a gruff voice from the doorway, a parade-ground voice. "Nate Mulligan, I swear to God, if you leave this house now, don't you *ever* even *think* about coming back."

Israfel opens his mouth blindly, paralyzed by this unanticipated turn of events. Nate, though, is quicker, opening the trunk under Israfel's hand and lifting the suitcase by its edge to toss it inside. "Get in the car," he says smartly, moving already toward the passenger door. "C'mon, Raf; *get in the car.*"

Israfel is accustomed enough to taking orders that the tone of Nate's voice reanimates him somewhat, propels him almost on autopilot back into the appropriate seat behind the wheel. "Your father—" he begins, fumbling with the keys.

"It's just typical Dad," Nate tells him curtly. He sounds irritated, but not in a way directed toward Israfel. "Five minutes ago he was throwing me out in no uncertain terms. Now he's telling me to get the hell back in there. So he can, what, give me a good hiding?" He snorts. "Yeah, right. He's all bark. Just *drive*."

Israfel glances cautiously out of the passenger side window. Captain Mulligan is on his way across the lawn, apparently in the direction of his truck. "Dear God," Israfel mutters under his voice as he puts the car in drive, "*please* tell me I'm not about to be driven out of town in some kind of madcap car chase."

Nate throws his head back and laughs at that, reaching over to curl his hand around the nape of Israfel's neck. "You're kidding me, right? I wish he would. He can't do shit, now, you know. I *am* eighteen." He sounds more than amused—exhilarated, rather—and the warmth of his hand seems to bleed right into Israfel's bones. He laughs a little, too, and pushes the pedal to the floor.

By the time they reach the end of the block, it's pretty clear that Captain Mulligan is not intent on following them. Nate seems mildly disappointed, but not at all surprised. "Typical Dad," he repeats, with a wave of his hand. "He's always threatening these incredible punishments, but he very rarely follows through."

"What happened in there?" Israfel asks cautiously. They're nearing the freeway now, almost in the clear. He eases off the pedal a little, feeling his heartbeat slowing back to something closer to normal.

"Pretty much what I expected," Nate says. His arm is still lying across the back of Israfel's seat, fingers curled loosely around his shoulder. It's nice, reassuring, and Israfel feels he could drive like this forever.

"Mm?" he prompts, most of his attention on the traffic.

"Oh, you know." Nate shrugs. "Said my goodbyes to Tommy first, and then sent him upstairs out of the way of things before I made my little announcement. Mom cried. Said what did I *mean* I was gay, how did I *know*. Why would I *do* this to her."

"You're not gay," Israfel feels compelled to point out. Nate makes a disparaging sound in his nose.

"Believe me, Raf, you don't want to start tryin' to explain that shit to my mom. If I'd said I still liked girls, she'd just have asked why I couldn't ignore the other bit and go find a nice girl."

Israfel hrrrms his agreement. "Very likely." He smiles a little, the corner of his mouth lifting. "So what did you say to all that?"

"Said I was in love with a guy," Nate explains casually, as if it's nothing. His tone is light, but Israfel's stomach twists a little in sympathy, knowing the sort of man Nate is, the way he's been brought up. His self-confidence is all Captain Mulligan, even where they disagree on what, exactly, is worth being confident about. He has an inherited reticence, too, when it comes to these sorts of declarations. Nate is fully capable of sentimentality, but very rarely does he articulate it.

"And what did she say?" Israfel prompts gently, his tone all understanding.

"Cried some more," Nate says, with a little sigh. "But she'll get over it. I mean, honestly, she will. Dad kind of let her say her piece before he weighed in with all his 'no son of mine will be a faggot' speeches, but then he dragged out the old 'if you're gonna be like that, you can get the hell out of my house', which, you know." He shrugs. "Sort of led me nicely onto my little announcement."

Israfel laughs despite himself. "Clever. And?"

"I told him that was fine and dandy with me, because I was off to California, where I had a college place lined up." He laughs. "You should have seen their faces. Dad was all, 'who with?' and I asked him who he *thought*, and then he started yelling at me to get the hell out, then, and Mom started yelling at *him* to stop 'driving me away'." He grins ruefully, picking at a loose thread on the knee of his jeans. "I saw my chance to slip out and took it."

"Opportunist," Israfel chides him, but he can't help but smile. Nate seems shockingly unconcerned about the whole situation. Israfel had been bracing himself for far worse, for miles and miles of unhappiness and reassurances and determined endurance as the road rolled under their wheels. But Israfel knows the face of Nate's false

173

contentment, and this is absolutely not it. "You think they'll be all right about it?"

"Nothing they can do," Nate tosses back lightly. "And believe me, I've heard them arguing often enough to know how this fight is gonna end. Mom will guilt-trip Dad into thinking he's the reason she's lost her beautiful first-born son, holy moly golly gosh. Dad'll tell her it was 'all my own fault'. Then they'll accuse each other of being the reason that I 'turned out this way', and then Mom will trot out the first argument again. And so on until Dad's apologizing to *her* without even knowing how he got there, and then they'll decide that it's their duty to be nice to me if I should ever actually call, because they won't want me to just never call again." He shrugs. "I mean, they're bigoted backwater hicks, but they're my family. They're not gonna drop me altogether. Even if it takes a couple years."

"You know them best," Israfel concedes, glancing sidelong to smile at Nate.

Nate smiles back, mouth and eyes both softening. He looks away after a moment, reaches out to fiddle with the car stereo. "Well, whatever," he says gruffly, over the sound of white noise on the radio. "Doesn't matter anyway. I could go out of my way to keep them happy, but that's not exactly my priority any more. They'd like me to stay here and rot, and that's not what I want."

"What do you want?" Israfel asks softly, eyes still on Nate's face. He stretches out a hand, touches the backs of his fingers to Nate's cheekbone. Nate shivers a little at the touch, closes his eyes briefly.

"I want...." Nate glances up and over at him, mouth curving up a little. There's a moment of silence sparking, heavy with promise between them. And then the white noise of the stereo suddenly bleeds over into sound as Nate twiddles the knob, blasting out something so incongruous Israfel has to laugh.

"That's what I want," Nate grins, sitting back in his seat.

"AC/DC?" Israfel teases, but he's still grinning, thumb stroking over Nate's jaw.

"AC/DC," Nate repeats firmly, but his cheeks are pink along the bone and he's biting his lip on an embarrassed grin.

"Okay," says Israfel, shrugging, and flicks the headlights onto full beam. The road ahead of them is likely to be empty for miles, and they've a long way to go before their first stop.

"Okay," Nate nods, throwing Israfel a smile, the glare of the lights glancing off his cat-green eyes.

He turns up the radio to something close to ear-splitting levels, but somehow Israfel can't bring himself to complain.

Twenty-one

TURNS out, Israfel is far more malleable a personality than he knew. For someone whose entire adult life has been spent moving from one bubble to another, he finds life in San Diego surprisingly easy to adapt to. The lack of rain is something entirely new to him, but it's one of the greatest perks of California, after the politics and the shockingly decent public school system.

The taxes on everything, Israfel could have done without, but he's far too aware of his own good fortune to complain about something as minor as that.

Their apartment is small, but it isn't too small for two, particularly given their complete lack of furniture. Lack of funds, too, means that this state of affairs continues for a while. They procure a double air mattress from Walmart, and Israfel apologizes profusely about it, but Nate only laughs and shrugs it off. "It's like camping," he says. "'Cept I don't have to freeze my balls off."

By the middle of February, Nate has somehow acquired a job in Starbucks. He spends a lot of time making jokes about it, but

Israfel is fully aware that, secretly, he's rather pleased. He gets free espresso whenever he feels the urge and is provided daily with entire lines of soy-latte-ordering West Coasters to laugh about.

The best thing about it for Nate, though, is that he knows it's only temporary. In May, Nate gets a whole slew of letters with official stamps, which Israfel stacks nervously on the kitchen table (procured second hand from a garage sale). Israfel is trying to write a book. He isn't getting very far with it, but he did have time to change Nate's address on all of his college applications, so there's no mystery about what all these letters are doing here.

Nate rips the letters open nonchalantly, but Israfel sees in his face that he's nervous. As it transpires, it's unnecessary. All of his colleges come back to him with offers, and two with full-ride scholarships. The fact that one of these is from UC San Diego puts a lot of Israfel's concerns to bed before he's even had to express them. Sometimes, it's almost as if there's an angel watching over them both.

By the time Nate starts at UCSD in the fall, Israfel has given up on his idle hope of becoming the Catholic Ernest Hemingway. This is mostly because a position was recently advertised at the local community college, seeking a lecturer in theology. Israfel applied for the role without any great hope of being considered, but the college seems to have different ideas about his suitability for the post. When the new semester rolls around, he and Nate are both starting at a new school, equal parts nervous and excited.

It's startling, really, how easily things fall into the new pattern. Israfel teaches four days a week and writes hopeful little articles on Fridays. Nate picks up a motorbike somewhere, paid for with the part of his scholarship that would have covered school accommodation, and uses it to flit between his classes, the apartment, and his job. They have breakfast together in the morning, make dinner together when they're both done for the day, and everything's so fucking perfect that sometimes Israfel thinks he must be dreaming. He's fallen down the rabbit hole, and this is what's beyond.

If it's a dream, he has no desire to wake up.

The seasons pass in their California way, everything auburn and gold. Before he knows it, Nate's twenty-one, and Israfel has to stop for a moment and literally count the years, shocked at how long it's been.

"Three years?" he laughs. "Three years? You have *got* to be kidding me."

"What, you want rid of me?" Nate sets his beer bottle down on the floor and climbs into Israfel's lap, leaning forward to rub his mouth wetly against his jaw.

"You're drunk," Israfel chides, but he's smiling, and Nate laughs in response.

"You're hot," he counters. "And before you ask, you're hot when I'm sober too."

"Sweet-talker," Israfel says, rolling his eyes elaborately. "Why on *earth* would I ever want rid of someone like you?"

"Too right," Nate says, and slips off Israfel's lap onto the floor.

One thing Israfel can say for the years is that they have somehow enabled Nate to refine his skill at fellatio. It's rather a coarse thought to have, but Israfel is two bottles of beer the lesser, mentally, and besides, it's absolutely true. Nate takes him deep to the back of his throat now, swallows around him as if it's the easiest thing in the world.

Israfel doesn't have much of a faculty left for thinking, after that.

The spring semester starts and finishes, all under the California sun. Israfel has actually contemplated picking up his novel again by the time July rolls around and his summer classes are few and far between. He's frowning at the first few chapters, now three years old, when an unfamiliar sound makes him glance up in surprise.

It takes him a minute or two to realize that it's the doorbell. Nobody rings their doorbell. They have a decent number of mutual friends, Nate's schoolmates and Israfel's colleagues, and other people they've met in their adventures in the wider world, but none of them ever rings. Israfel wonders idly if Nate has ordered something, wonders if they'll mind taking his signature for it instead. Nate, as far as he's aware, is still asleep, and Israfel isn't inclined to wake him.

He's got a little speech half composed when he opens the door, fully expecting to be confronted with a delivery guy of some sort.

The guy at the door doesn't seem to be carrying a package. As far as Israfel can tell, he isn't wearing a uniform, either, just a blue golf shirt under an open jacket, the kind of thing any college kid might wear. He's sort of familiar, too, as if Israfel's seen him somewhere before, but he can't for the life of him think where. He's ludicrously tall, with hair that must have been in dire need of a cut six months ago. Israfel furrows his brow for a moment, trying to place him.

"Hi," says the kid, spreading his arms in some strange sort of greeting. The gesture displays his impressive wingspan, but it doesn't really help Israfel.

"Sorry," he says slowly, tipping his head to the side to better study his visitor. "But I don't think I know you. You're not in my Theology 101, are you?"

The kid tips back his head and laughs, and suddenly Israfel catches a flash of something, some memory sparking, deep in the pit of his stomach. It's gone again in a second, though, and Israfel isn't any closer to remembering.

"Tom," says the kid, holding out an enormous paw of a hand. "It's me, Israfel. Tom."

Even then, the explanation takes a second to register. He doesn't know any Toms. As far as Israfel can remember, the only Tom he knows is Nate's little brother, and *that* boy is thirteen years old if he's a day, scrawny and cute and short enough to tuck under Israfel's arm.

"Mulligan," says Tom, the corner of his mouth twitching up in a way that, yes, is familiar, and holy Jesus God, yes it is.

"Sorry," Israfel gasps, when he's recovered his breath. "Oh, Tom, I'm so sorry. It's just that you're…." He gestures upward. Up, and up, and up. Tom laughs, scuffing his feet.

"Yeah, I know. Sorry." He has the grace to look sheepish about it. "Is Nate around?"

Nate is in bed, the sheets rucked up and twisted around his body until he resembles nothing so much as some kind of human burrito. Israfel gives up trying to find a way into the tangle after a moment's fruitless effort, shaking Nate by the shoulder instead.

"Nate," he hisses, shakes him again, cards his fingers through his hair. "Nate, get up."

"Huh?" Nate's never been terribly coherent when he first wakes up. He blinks up at Israfel blearily, his face soft with sleep.

"Your brother's here," Israfel tells him sharply, very aware of Tom in the next room. "Did you know about this?"

For a second, Nate only stares at him, uncomprehending. Then, "*Tommy's* here?"

Israfel nods briefly. "In the front room. And he's—"

But Nate is out of bed before Israfel is even finished speaking, bed hair and rumpled pajama pants be damned. He throws open the door, opens his mouth, and then closes it again stupidly.

"Hey, Nate," Tom says, in his new, deeper voice, from his new, ridiculous height.

"Jesus Christ," says Nate. "You've been cursed, like Tom Hanks in *Big*."

There's an awkward half a beat of silence, and Israfel feels an edge of concern looming. But then Tom laughs, and Nate starts laughing, too, and that's enough for him.

"Yeah," says Tom. "Yeah, I, uh. I guess you could see it that way."

"Bitch," says Nate, and he crushes Tom to him like he'll blow away, otherwise; like he's bound to disappear any second. Tom only closes his eyes and holds his big brother back, leaning (unbelievably) down into his tenacious grasp.

Tom has a full-ride scholarship to Stanford. They ascertain this fact over black coffee while Israfel putters about the kitchen putting together enough waffle mix to satisfy two overgrown young men, plus himself. Tom's only seventeen, to the best of Israfel's recollection—Tom confirms, when asked, that he did, indeed, turn seventeen this past May—but then, he always was the cleverest Mulligan.

Given that Nate has managed to keep up his scholarship at UCSD for the past three years, without any apparent difficulty at all, Israfel finds this assertion a little ridiculous, but Nate seems entirely unbothered by it.

"Mom always meant to get Tommy off to college a year early," he recalls, stuffing a forkful of waffle into his mouth. "Never thought she'd let you this far out of her sight, though, kiddo."

Tom smiles, shrugging his shoulders as he takes the proffered glass of orange juice from Israfel's hand. "I have you to thank for that," he says.

Nate raises his eyebrows. "Me?"

"Stanford's only four hundred miles from here," Tom points out. "I never gave Mom and Dad your actual address, but you sent them Christmas cards, Nate. They know you're living in San Diego. And when you're that far away, I guess California kind of sounds smaller than it is."

"Yeah, *only* four hundred miles," Nate says, but he's smiling. Nate could manage that much in a day, easily, as Israfel is only too well aware. It's certainly a great improvement on two thousand miles, and all the weeks it took to cover that distance when they drove out here in the first place.

"They knew you were coming to visit Nate, then?" Israfel strives to keep his tone neutral as he pours orange juice into his own glass, but he isn't sure how far he's managed it.

"Sure," Tom says, nodding. "And you, I guess. I mean, they don't agree with it, but...." He shrugs. "I guess it was always a given that I'd side with Nate. They didn't exactly try to change my mind."

"Knew it was pointless, probably," Nate says, reaching over the table to ruffle Tom's hair. Tom makes a strangled noise of irritation and ducks his head away, but Israfel doesn't miss the smile tugging at his mouth.

"Probably," he says, slopping maple syrup over his waffle. "You brainwashed me young."

"Better me than them," says Nate airily.

Tom's smile doesn't dim, but the tone of his reply isn't light, holds a certain gratitude in it that Israfel hopes Nate can hear. "Damn right, Nate," Tom says. "Thank God for you."

This is a sentiment that Israfel can most certainly get behind.

They put Tom up on the air mattress they bought when they first arrived here, now habitually stuffed into the cupboard under the stairs. The act of inflating it is something of a nostalgic one for Israfel, and he and Nate exchange more than a couple of looks as they stretch a fitted sheet over the contraption.

Later, in their own bed (IKEA's best, thank you) Israfel pulls Nate against him, fits himself neatly to the curves and lines of Nate's back.

"Life's weird, huh?" he whispers into the soft space behind Nate's ear.

Nate laughs, pulls Israfel's arm across his waist and slots their fingers together. "Weird, how?"

"Well." Israfel wriggles a little, working Nate's ankles apart with his foot and then slotting his own ankle between them. "Weird like your brother suddenly showing up on our doorstep weird."

"Hmm." Nate's smiling, his soft sound of assent vibrating with it. "How about weird like my tiny kid brother suddenly being eight feet tall weird?"

Israfel laughs. "You didn't expect that, huh?"

Nate snorts and shakes his head. "I mean, we've been in touch, you know that. But it's not like he said, 'oh, hey, by the way, Nate, I'm growing at a totally ridiculous rate. Thought you'd like to know'."

"He wanted to surprise you," Israfel teases, scraping his thumbnail over the soft flesh of Nate's belly, just under the hem of his shirt. The touch makes Nate squirm back against him in protest, as Israfel knew it would.

"*Stop* it," he cautions, and then, "If he did, he did a damn good job of it."

Israfel smiles against the nape of his neck. Nate smells good here, all soft musk and shampoo and linen, and Israfel rubs his open mouth over the knob of bone for a moment, curling his tongue around it lazily. Nate wriggles in his arms, makes a soft sound of approval.

"Guess he'll have to be your Big Little Brother, now," Israfel observes slyly. His fingers edge under the waistband of Nate's pajama pants, stroking back and forth over the paper-fine skin. "Which, I suppose, makes you the Little Big Brother."

Nate's breath punches out of him on a harsh little gasp, fingers sliding down to pin Israfel's hand at his hip. "Jesus Christ, Raf," he gets out, "*Whatever*, okay? But I will seriously, *seriously* give you anything you want if you stop talking about my kid brother while you're doing that, all right?" He releases his grip on Israfel's hand slowly, pushes it unsubtly lower. "Seriously. *God.*"

"I prefer Raf," Israfel comments blithely, hand curling loose around the base of Nate's cock. Nate hisses, arches back into Israfel's body, and it's just as good as it ever was, watching him move like that, watching him react to Israfel's touch. It makes him feel powerful, blessed and privileged and hot all over, and Nate has given this feeling no reason to lessen.

"Raf, huh?" Nate murmurs, tipping his head back onto Israfel's shoulder. It's an unspoken signal between them, this baring of his throat an invitation from Nate, and Israfel gladly takes him up on it, licking a wet trail from the junction of neck and shoulder up to the fine skin behind Nate's ear. Nate wriggles beautifully under the attention, and Israfel rocks up against his backside, making his pleasure unquestionably felt.

"Raf," he confirms, nipping at the lobe of Nate's ear. "You think you've got that?"

"Raf," Nate pants, fucking into his hand, "*Raf!*"

It's partly a response, partly an involuntary sound, coaxed out of Nate by Israfel's fingers on his cock, his thumb slipping over the crown. It's partly, even, a tease, but mostly it's a confirmation, an obvious manifestation of something Israfel never thought he'd have, never thought he deserved. Mostly, it's Nate just *getting* him, without the need for explanation. It's Nate being here with him, really with him, the way he was in the dreams Israfel once thought could never exist beyond the realms of fantasy. It's having an apartment and a job and a significant other that he loves, that he wants, that he knows from the inside out. It's having this life that so many people take for granted, but which Israfel never thought he could ever have.

He can't believe, sometimes, that he was ever so stupid. When he's moving sleepily around the kitchen before Monday morning school, pouring out the old milk in the sink while Nate ducks under his arm to press a kiss to his mouth, he can't even imagine how something so normal could be thought of as "wrong." They're *ridiculously* normal, he and Nate. It's disgusting. The girl at the video rental place makes no secret of the fact that she thinks they're the cutest couple she's ever seen. The guy who works maintenance on the apartment building refers to Nate as "that handsome boy of yours" without even a suggestion of sarcasm. At first, it felt like a dream world, but Israfel knows better now. Now he knows it's the old world that wasn't real—the world where rules were more important than reality, and the way Nate's hand fits in his was somehow evil.

Tom stays with them for the better part of a week. They take him to the zoo and out to Coronado Island. They drive him out along the coastal road, with the windows rolled down so the salt breeze whips through their hair. By the end of the day, Tom looks rather as if he's been dragged backwards through foliage, but as far as Israfel's concerned, that's a matter entirely between him and his ludicrous volume of hair. He seems to have enjoyed himself, regardless, and that's the important thing.

When he sets off for Palo Alto, the apartment seems oddly quiet. It's not surprising, really. Constant chatter sort of came as a natural result of Nate's long separation from his brother, and the aftermath of anything that intense always feels strange. But Israfel feels a little drained, a little out of place, as he leans against the windowsill, watching the streams of cars criss-crossing like caterpillars of light.

"Hey," Nate says. His voice is soft, but he's smiling, like he knows what Israfel's feeling without even asking. He slips an arm around Israfel's waist, leans into him in the narrow window cavity.

Of course he knows what Israfel's thinking. Nate always does.

"You gonna be okay?" Israfel asks quietly, into Nate's soft hair. There's more of it than there used to be. Nate will probably get it cut soon. Israfel isn't entirely sure that he wants him to. It's nice like this, sweet-smelling and warm when he buries his face in it.

"Mmm," Nate says. He leans up to press a kiss to the corner of Israfel's mouth. "Nice to know we'll actually be able to see each other from time to time. Tom could come here over the vacations, maybe?"

"Sure," Israfel agrees, turning slightly to catch Nate's mouth in a kiss. "If he doesn't want to go see your parents."

"It's a helluva ways out there," Nate reasons. He twists his fingers in Israfel's belt loops, pulling him close. "And hey, we have a home here, right? There's no need to go all the way out to the East Coast looking for one, with us here."

Israfel laughs softly, carding his fingers through Nate's hair. "Yeah, we do," he concedes. Nate smells like soap, like coffee, with an edge of warm skin. The apartment around them is still small, a little cramped, but it's theirs, now: their living room, their kitchen, their bed. The dishes are theirs, the pictures on the walls, the books. It's something Israfel never expected, something that feels like a gift every day.

"Yeah," he says again. "We have a home here."

Nate smiles, curve of his lips tangible against skin. "Imagine that," he says, voice dark laced with amusement.

"Don't have to," Israfel tells him lightly. "Not anymore."

He disentangles himself then, heading toward the kitchen without looking back, but he doesn't need to see Nate's face to know exactly which smile he's wearing. They know each other far too well for that.

An avid reader of everything from New Scientist to the back of the cereal box, LOUISE BLAYDON has been writing, encouraged by her father, ever since she could hold a pen. Her writing, like her reading, has wandered erratically from genre to genre, but has settled firmly on gay romance, to the mild bemusement of Dad. Louise also writes sporadically for various journalistic publications and has been known to print the occasional poem.

She owes much of her inspiration and support these days to an amazing network of friends, whose willingness to listen to her rail against life, the universe, and everything she could not live without. Louise's pursuits beyond writing are worryingly few, chief among them being Worrying About Not Having Pursuits Beyond Writing. However, this has long been the case, and after many abortive attempts to pad her leisure-time resume with everything from hiking to yoga, she has pretty much given up. She does enjoy singing, country walking, making deep-voiced sardonic remarks, and tasting the rain, but has a horror of organized activities.

Louise has altogether too many academic qualifications and can only dream that her list of published works will one day be equally long.

Also by LOUISE BLAYDON

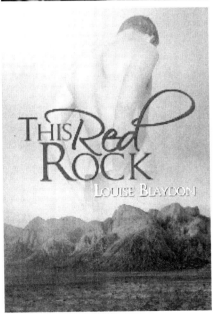

http://www.dreamspinnerpress.com